THE CATALAN CONNECTION

a spy novel

Max Mitkevicius

camembert roti....

"Imperare sibi maximum imperium est." Seneca

SAN PEDRO, BELIZE

C old beer, hot sun, and a blue-green sea. It was all Peter Strickland ever needed. Sitting in the shade of the thatched palapa, it was hard to imagine life getting any easier. Belize had a way of doing that to you after a while. Maybe it was the one-dollar Belikin beer or the dirt cheap, fresh lobster dinners. Whatever it was, the laid back English speaking country had a way of making all your troubles drift away with the ocean-fresh breeze. Pete Strickland was one man who definitely needed it.

It had taken two full weeks on San Pedro to get

to where Pete was now – comfortable, and relaxed enough to throw back a few beers before noon and not worry about missing something. Here there was nothing to miss. Except maybe the Wednesday night chicken bingo competition, where sun-chapped tourists bet over the location of chicken droppings in a numbered grid. It takes a fair amount of alcohol to get excited about where a chicken's going to shit next, but with a decent enough buzz the spectacle can be surprisingly entertaining.

But that's about all that was on Pete's schedule. And for once, the chronically overworked and slightly disheveled Peter Strickland was all too happy to sit back, drink, and not have a care in the world. They couldn't get to him here. No phone, no internet – he hadn't even let them know where he was staying – just "I'll be in Belize, see you in three weeks." It felt good to be out of touch. Nothing could bother him. Or so he thought.

Pete had spent most of that early October day lazily stretched out in a cheap plastic lounger perched on the rooftop of the crumbling cinder-block hotel where he was staying down by the water taxi terminal. It definitely wasn't the Ritz, and had a certain 'down on your luck' kind of feel to it. But the views from the roof were good, and the rooms only cost twenty dollars a night. More importantly though, it was just the sort of place where Pete had always felt most comfortable. Just like the redneck riviera beach towns on Florida's Gulf Coast where he grew up, here there were no pretensions.

Around a quarter to three in the afternoon, after the compulsory cheeseburger in paradise, and with the still far-off smell of rain in the air, Pete decided to make the 15 minute trek down the road to Angelita's, an idyllic collection of cabanas lining San Pedro's coast where the higher-end tourists liked to stay and the normally priced dollar beers cost about five. Overpriced, yes...but Angelita's had it all. There was a shaded lagoon pool that was perfect for lounging with a cold beverage in the tropical heat. And down at the shoreline, a private dock with all the amenities to enjoy Belize's spectacular coastline and the Western Hemisphere's longest reef. If you were in San Pedro and had money to spare, this was the ideal spot to throw it away.

Pete ambled through the pastel-coloured bungalows and out to the hotel bar near the water's edge. He was just about to order a drink when he spotted a familiar looking face just off to his left, sitting at the end of a row of empty chairs.

Pete grimaced. In his line of work it was never good to see a familiar face. It usually meant only one thing: vacation over.

He walked down to the edge of the bar and took a seat next to the man with a big, bushy moustache.

Max Mitkevicius

A strong breeze began to kick up, rustling the palm fronds overhead and scattering sand over the wood decked floor. And for a few moments there were no words between them.

Then his old friend Angel Hernandez smiled. "So what are we drinking?"

Pete nodded, then waggled two fingers in the bartender's direction.

"Two cold ones."

The pony-tailed bartender, ever attentive, cracked open two long-necked brown bottles and poured the malty contents into a couple of opaquely frosted mugs, fresh from the freezer.

"Muy bueno," Hernandez said, admiring the handiwork. "This is a classy place, hombre. Must be a big change for a guy like you."

"A guy like me? What's that supposed to mean?"

"You know what it means."

Pete shot Hernandez a hard glance, trying to be serious. Then they both broke out laughing.

"You know I like you Angel, I really do." Pete said, as he gave Hernandez a hearty slap across the back. Then he gripped his friend's shoulder tight, not really joking anymore.

"Now why don't you tell me what the hell you're

doing here?"

Angel Hernandez took a big sip of beer, the foam coating his Magnum P.I. style moustache.

"OK, OK amigo...keep your shirt on. Let's finish these cold *cervezas* before I ruin your vacation."

"Ahhhhh," Pete sighed, squinting his eyes for added effect. "Just like old times."

Angel Hernandez had worked with Pete since the beginning – back when they were just a couple of fresh-faced kids looking for adventure. They'd come from different backgrounds sure, but in the end, they were just the same: two cowboys, pushing the envelope like young guns should. They'd had their fair share of laughs on those first few assignments together. And they certainly tested a lot of boundaries. But they never crossed the line.

Until one day they did.

They had left North Africa years ago under a cloud of recriminations and uncertainty, Pete transferred to a headquarters job back in Washington while Hernandez was assigned to a smuggling operation out in the Baltic Sea.

But they had stayed close in spite of the professional distance that had been forced upon them, and it was easy to fall back into that old comforting rhythm of playful one-upmanship.

But behind all of the camaraderie and good-natured ribbing, there was something deeper that bound them together.

It had been a while since they'd seen each other, and as they hunched over the bar and caught up, Pete couldn't help but notice that Angel Hernandez didn't look good.

His face was unusually pale and his once dark moustache was now flecked with grey. There were deep purple circles under his tired brown eyes, and there was a certain sadness in the way his shoulders slumped slightly forward. He seemed drained somehow - and much older than his 42 years. The operation in the Baltic had clearly done a number on him.

Or maybe it was something else.

"Listen Pete," Hernandez said, his tone turning suddenly serious as he finished his beer. "We need to talk."

Pete's gaze narrowed, a hint of anxiety creeping into his consciousness for the first time in a fortnight. He tried his best to stay calm, but his eyes betrayed him.

"What's up?"

"Not here. Let's take a walk."

The white sand crunched under their feet as they

walked down the narrow strip of beach on the water's edge. You could see the waves breaking on the reef less than a mile out. It really was paradise. Unfortunately for Peter Strickland, the nastiness of real life was about to ruin this elysian mirage.

"Nobody knows I'm here yet - I came as soon as I heard," Hernandez said, quietly surveying the fast-moving storm clouds gathering on the darkening horizon. "There's a name coming out of Europe."

A blue flash of lightning lit up the sky way out in the distance, and Pete felt his stomach clench slightly, his body's response to the palpable sense of danger, as yet unspoken.

But he already knew.

The Catalan was back.

EL RAVAL, BARCELONA, SPAIN

Tucked quaintly into a shaded-doorway on Carrer de Carme in the old Barrio Chino neighbourhood of Barcelona was Shalimar restaurant. The epitome of a neighbourhood joint in this predominantly Pakistani enclave, Shalimar served the best *Bindi Tori* in the city. Arnau Leport was enjoying just that delicacy, sitting at a small table next to an intricately tiled wall. A Cobra beer sat perched next to his dish of spicy sautéed okra, soaking the paper tablecloth with the dripping condensation formed from the hot, stagnant air. The scent of fried onions, dewy and sweet, would certainly permeate the fabric of his clothing, but none of that mattered because if there was a culinary heaven for Leport, then this was it.

Tall and lanky with the musculature of a dedicated yoga practitioner, Leport was a man of simple, and for the most part, spartan tastes. But here, in the confines of Shalimar, he allowed himself an altogether rare moment of self-indulgence.

Yet even in this, there was a methodical sort of dedication.

A bite of okra, a slug of beer, and a quick back-of-the-hand wipe across a sweaty forehead formed the rhythm of his ritual. The burn steadily increasing in intensity with every mouthful until broken from necessity by a salve of the spongy garlic naan bread followed by a sip of ice-cold beer. Sweating profusely from the abundance of hot pepper (per his request), Leport revelled in the near mystical ecstasy of a spice induced endorphin rush coupled with alcoholic intoxication. It was, indeed, a sacred brew.

A little dizzy from the riot of sensations and fully engaged in the sanctity of the meal, Leport didn't notice the stooped old man who had quietly moved into the table behind him.

"Es troba" whispered the grizzled, sun beaten gentleman.

It is found.

It was an immediate wake-up call for Leport, who put down his fork, laid down twenty euros on the small table and silently walked out the curtained front door and onto the cobbled, winding streets of the old town.

Passing the palm studded Rambla del Raval and heading towards the ocean, Leport ran a hand through his close-cropped dark hair and calmly switched SIM cards in his phone before catching a taxi directly to Barcelona's El Prat Airport.

ROME, ITALY

The small dining room at Hostaria da Giovanni was packed with the usual lunch crowd. Locals from the Trastevere neighbourhood who knew where to go for the best deal around converged on Giovanni's precisely at twelve thirty to secure one of about ten tiny, cramped tables. Arriving late and having to wait was dangerous, as the availability of every item on the daily-changing menu diminished with each passing hour. At Giovanni's, unlike almost every other restaurant in Rome, there were no tourists and the anonymous façade protected the dingy interior from the Vatican hordes that occasionally wandered away from St. Peter's and down Via della Lungara. It was the ideal spot for Stefano to recommend a lunch meeting, especially since he worked a block away at the local prison – less walking time meant more time for *pranzo*, Italy's version of an extended lunch, wine included.

For Mark Vashtan though, this was actually a nightmare of a spot for a meeting. The tight space and homogeneity of the crowd meant he was sure to stand out. There were no alternate entrances or exits and no way to avoid being noticed by staff and patrons alike. The location violated just about every rule of tradecraft that Vashtan could imagine.

Yet still here he was, pushed up close against the wall under a hanging celeste-coloured scarf from the SS Lazio soccer team and trying desperately not to look like an idiot as he fumbled with a huge plate of spaghetti al sugo.

Stefano sat across from him, delicately twirling his fettuccine with one hand and pouring two glasses of vino rosso from the carafe on the table with the other.

"*Senti,*" Stefano mumbled as he washed back a mouthful of pasta with the acrid Frascati table wine. "Listen. I have some information. *Per te,* for you, it could be very interesting."

Stefano had been Vashtan's contact for over a year

now ever since the Rome station realised that Italy's victims of the war on terrorism usually ended up at the Regina Coeli prison.

North Africans had long been arriving on Italy's open coastlines to search for jobs and a better life. Recently, large numbers had been coming as part of the global jihadist movement. Setting up shop had proven fairly easy for these radical operatives - especially given Italy's notoriously lax criminal system. Only recently had law enforcement really cracked down. After all, it wasn't long ago that organised crime was the biggest threat here. But these days neither the Sicilian Mafia, the Neapolitan Camorra, nor the Calabrian 'Ndrangheta were beheading tourists or threatening to invade Rome.

So now the formerly freely-operating terrorist cells were slowly being rounded up and sent to stay at Regina Coeli – where Stefano Fratelli kept a close eye on the offenders as chief guard for the Islamic ward.

Privy to the inmate chatter and fluent in Arabic (his father had sold refrigerators in Libya when Stefano was young - before Gaddafi expropriated all his family's assets), Stefano was a goldmine of intelligence for Vashtan and probably his most prized agent. The information Stefano had passed along was far more valuable than any of the interrogations currently in progress at the various and far-flung secret prisons known simply as 'black sites,' and had proven accurate time and time again. It certainly helped that none of the prisoners knew that Stefano could speak and understand Arabic. But what Stefano was about to say this time was of a far greater magnitude than anything Vashtan could have imagined.

"Have you ever heard the name Arnau Leport?"

"What did you just say?"

"Leport. Arnau Leport."

Vashtan's face immediately went a few shades lighter as he put down his forkful of poorly twisted spaghetti and looked around frantically for the single disinterested waiter.

"*Il conto, per favore.*"

BELIZE CITY, BELIZE

Angel Hernandez hated Belize City. In his opinion it was just another dirty, hot, overcrowded Central American shit-hole - - and too much like the places he had struggled so hard to get away from as a kid. All the cruise ships, the crappy hotels, and low-level festering street crime meant this sweaty backwater was decidedly not on his list of ideal stop-overs. But he hadn't come for pleasure, and at least he'd given his friend Pete half a chance to get out of this mess alive. He'd done his duty. Now it was time to go.

Pete Strickland, on the other hand, always enjoyed the city. It wasn't flashy or modern, the beaches were nonexistent, and the local cuisine was less than stunning - - but there was something real about this place. It had a visceral feeling to it, from the crumbling shacks near the bus terminal, to the old colonial administrative buildings that had certainly seen better days. Belize City was a place that wasn't trying to trick you with flashiness (well, except for the phoney cruise ship terminal area, which was pretty much just a goddamn phoney cruise ship terminal). For the most part though, the city was simply a rough, swelteringly hot, jumping-off spot for somewhere else. But this suited Pete Strickland just fine. It was a perfect place to grab a beer and watch the world go by in quiet anonymity. At least that was normally the case.

Today, however, Pete had a one-way ticket to Melchor in his hand, a potential surveillance team to evade, and plenty of unpleasantness on his mind.

After a high-speed jaunt on a water taxi (paid handsomely to cruise through the mangroves and then quickly double back to the port), a circuitously sweaty walk through the downtown markets, and a quick and disgustingly bitter coffee in a dilapidated old social club near the dried up canal, Pete shook Angel's hand one last time, bidding his friend a silent farewell. Then he hopped on board the bluebird bus line for the bone jarring ride to Melchor de Mencos on the Guatemala border.

He was fairly certain he hadn't been followed, especially since the only other passengers on board appeared to be chicken farmers and a couple of hippie backpackers who smelled like the backside of a Moroccan camel.

Hard to fake that distinct aroma.

A car would have been infinitely quicker and more comfortable than the ratty old school bus with the busted out tail lights and lack of air conditioning, but this was really the only way to travel on the down-low.

It took about twenty minutes to wind through the chaotic traffic and make it out of town and onto the pot-holed roads that led to the Mayan jungle. Pete grimaced at the thought of what potentially lay ahead...flea-bag motels, sweaty underwear, greasy food-stalls. And for what? To end up having your fingernails pulled out and then a bullet to the back of the head?

And that's if you were lucky.

But really, what were the alternatives?

He closed his eyes, pulled a baseball cap low over his tangled and greying curly brown hair, and tried not to focus on the loose chicken that had taken an unusual interest in his fraying jeans.

Only 3 hours to the border...

FLORENCE, ITALY

Vashtan made the 90 minute trip from Rome's Termini station to Florence on the high speed *Freccia Rossa* train, in 2nd class. His youthful appearance dictated that he travel like a struggling academic in dingy jeans, a nondescript grey sweatshirt and white canvas Superga trainers. He preferred the free prosecco and extra space in the business compartment where the staff would address him as '*avvocato*' - the rough Italian equivalent of Esquire. Instead, it was cattle class and a window seat crammed next to a grungy, rather ripe smelling student.

He wished he'd gone to law school.

Disembarking at Santa Maria Novella station, it was a quick walk past the Mercato Centrale, pushing through the hordes at the outdoor stalls where unsuspecting tourists bought 'vera pelle' jackets and backpacks - "made in Italy!" shouted the brown-skinned vendors - straight from the port at Livorno, via China of course.

From Piazza San Marco, Vashtan hopped on the number 7 bus that would take him to his destination. It was a fifteen minute ride out of the centro storico and up the hill to Fiesole. Vashtan passed the stop at San Domenico with its run-of-the-mill pizzeria, a favourite hangout of students and staff from the international European University, then continued up the winding road with its increasingly stunning vistas of the city stretching out below - the heart of the Renaissance: the Duomo, the Uffizi, the David, and countless other treasures. A city of culture. A city of art.

The Via Beato Angelico continued snaking up, past the cypress-studded palazzi of Europe's new royalty. Instead of Medici, Ferragamo. Italy's own Beverley Hills.

The end of the line was Fiesole's main square, where Vashtan got out along with a few German tourists in black socks and sandals and an American couple who were arguing about whether on not they should have tipped their waiter at last night's dinner.

It was 30 minutes until his meeting with The Professor, so Vashtan walked up the street past the antique shops and quaint B&B's to the ARCI Fiesole, the communist social club, and ordered a negroni sbagliato (prosecco instead of gin), sat on the terrace overlooking the gentle rolling hills of the Colline Fiesolana, and waited.

EL COTILLO, FUERTEVENTURA

A warm ocean breeze gently ruffled the long translucent beige curtains of a tall window, filling the room with the faint scent of banana and coconut. There was a palm tree and lonely arid mountains in the distance, set against the pink-hued sky of early morning. Over the steady undulating roar of the sea, birds sang, and a single dog let out an occasional salute. A camper van rolled slowly by on the narrow street below, surfboards stacked on the roof, bone white and smooth-looking but for the aggressive multi-coloured fins curving up and out, waiting to cut through the massive swells crashing on the rocks off the north shore of Fuerteventura.

Arnau Leport stood in the window and drank his

dark, bitter coffee. A few grains of sand crunched under his bare feet on the smooth white tiles. In a few hours, the little town of El Cotillo would rumble to life with surfers, expats, fisherman, and lost souls. By midday, the smell of fried fish would waft through the cobbled alleys of the old port. But for now all was tranquil and calm.

Down at the harbour, a light skiff was getting fuelled up for what seemed to be a long excursion. The local owner had gotten a call a few nights before, prices had been arranged, and a fat sum of euros had arrived in his bank account the next morning. A sum generous enough that no questions would be asked.

Four *bocadillo* sandwiches of local *queso de cabra*, six cans of anchovy-stuffed olives, three metal tins of sardines packed in brine, two litres of water and two squat bottles of Portuguese *vinho verde* were all loaded on board. The GPS system had been disabled (again, no questions).

When the tall, lanky bearded man with close-cropped dark hair arrived an hour later there was barely an exchange of brusque 'buenas' and nodded heads - an unspoken agreement that all was in order. The bearded man climbed on board, fired up the outboard motor and navigated his non-descript little boat past the other old dingy vessels that bobbed and swayed under the crumbling ruins of an ancient stone fortification that stood watch over the protected cove.

Soon, Arnau Leport would be at sea, the Moroccan coastline of Africa unseen in the distance.

FIESOLE, TUSCANY

A few dark, grey clouds had started to dot the horizon over the olive-tree covered hills in the distance, and a cool, wet breeze was sweeping down over Monte Ceceri to the south, as Vashtan finished his drink and pulled a light blue wool scarf from his small leather satchel. It was autumn in Tuscany and a storm was brewing.

Fiesole was windier and colder than the city clustered around the curving Arno river below. Vashtan was sure that in winter it must be frigid and harsh. But for now it was just damp and chilly as he made his way down a narrow alley and toward the villa where *'il Professore'* had made his residence in a small independent cottage surrounded by a rather grand English-style garden. The cottage had most likely been used as servant quarters, back in the days when the old Villa was home to some noble family or other. Nowadays, however, most of the villa was rented out by the absentee Swiss owners, preferably to short-term tenants who didn't mind paying the exorbitant rental fees that were the going rate these days. The Professor was an exception though, and had been in the property for years now - but the owners didn't mind, as he always paid his rent on time (like clockwork…a big positive in Swiss eyes), he was quiet, and spent much of his time apparently abroad, always closing tight the forest-green Persian shutters of his front doors and windows.

Vashtan rung the top of four buzzers outside the massive wrought-iron gate on the steep road outside. The outsized stone cobbles were covered in a thin layer of bright green moss, slick with moisture. Vashtan checked his footing and rang again. As he turned to examine the unkempt block of Etruscan ruins on his left, covered with weeds and long since forgotten, there was a faint click and the steel coloured gate swung slowly, partially open with the distinctive creak that is particular to old, rusty gates.

Walking into the courtyard, small pebbles crunched underfoot and glistened in the fresh rain. Vashtan spotted the Professor down a garden path, standing under an ivy-covered pergola, his back turned, a charcoal coloured Aquascutum trench-coat with the collar turned up high. There was a an open bottle of Chianti on a stone table, and two small glasses.

In truth, *il Professore* was a shadowy figure, enveloped in mystery, and shrouded by the enigma of intertwining conspiracies that formed the backbone of Italy's postwar history. He was an old man now, and leaned just a bit on his acacia-wood cane, but still wielded considerable power, though perhaps waning (according to some) in this new world order. His hazel green eyes sparkled with intelligence behind vintage wire-rimmed spectacles that rested high on his long, thin nose. An elegant, curving scar marked his left cheek - a testament to his brief captivity by 'comrades' long ago during Italy's unruly and tragic *Anni di Piombo* - or Years of Lead. No one truly knew the Professor's story, and perhaps no one ever would. But for now, the Professor was Vashtan's best hope to understand the events now unfolding with the reappearance of his old nemesis Arnau Leport. Silent for five years, and now back in the game.

But why??

Il Professore poured out two glasses of the dark wine that smelled faintly of irises and lavender, and handed one to Vashtan as he approached. The Professor took off his spectacles, cleaning them gently on his yellow silk tie, and stared off aimlessly into the darkening horizon.

"Shall we begin?"

THE ATLANTIC

S alah hunched up against the curving interior of his low wooden fishing boat, closed
his eyes and listened to the gentle waves
lapping against the exterior hull. It was dark outside, a low mist snuffing out the light of the moon
and stars that normally shone brightly out here
off the coast of southern Morocco. A warm breeze
was blowing in off the Sahara, and a few drops of
perspiration dotted Salah's brow. He was falling
asleep.

Salah had already shut down the motor and
flipped on the transponder that he had received
in Marrakesh by the well-dressed men who had

given him his instructions. So far, everything had gone to plan. His long taxi ride from the bus depot out to the coastal resort of Essaouira had been fairly uneventful, the old Datsun with the Christmas lights twinkling wildly on the dashboard and the snuff-snorting driver didn't seem to interest the guards at the lone police checkpoint. Upon arrival, he had tracked down the marina owner as instructed, and paid in cash for the items on his list.

Now here he was, bobbing gently out at sea, waiting to hand off the small, tightly-taped package tucked deep in his left jacket pocket.

'An easy way to make money' thought Salah, now half-asleep.

The gentle hum of a motor churning in the distance roused him from his resting spot, and he hurriedly turned on the twin red and green lights that alternated in quick succession on the dash of his vessel. A signal.

Another low fishing boat slowly chugged toward Salah, with a dark-haired, bearded man at the helm.

'It must be him'

Salah raised both of his long, skinny arms over his head and waved them back and forth in a big, broad arching motion.

'Over here.'

Leport did not need the signal. After all, the transponder had led him to this precise spot, and the twin lights had confirmed that this was the ship he was looking for. "Imbecile," he mumbled softly to himself.

Leport steered his boat up alongside Salah and tossed out a thick twisted rope which Salah grabbed to pull the two boats tightly side by side.

There were no introductions.

"Do you have it?" Leport demanded.

Salah flashed a mostly toothless grin, the red and green lights illuminating his pock-marked face sharply from one side, and fished out the palm-sized parcel from his pocket. "And the money?"

Leport tossed a plastic shopping bag Salah's way. He caught it in mid-air, glanced inside, and shot another gaping grin at Leport, this time wider. Salah handed over the package, then turned to untie the rope from its binding. As he turned back towards Leport, with the words "thank you, my brother" barely out of his mouth, Salah saw a blinding flash of light. And then nothing.

Leport steadied the small caliber, black-matte Walther P22 that he had purchased from his favourite armoury in Villedecans on the outskirts of Barcelona many years ago, and calmly fired a second shot into Salah's already lifeless body. He then slipped the pistol into his coat and watched Salah slowly drift off with the current.

"*De res*. You're welcome...my brother"

FIESOLE, TUSCANY

The Professor sat at his small, spartan wooden desk, and watched through the big double-windows that looked out over the courtyard, as Vashtan walked hurriedly through the rain toward the slate-coloured steel gate and the world beyond.

Tapping absentmindedly on the glass face of his oversized Panerai diving watch, he let out an extended sigh, and allowed himself a rare moment of contentment.

He knew that he had told Vashtan just enough to set him in motion, like some wind-up toy marching mindlessly forward in perfect predictability. It would only be a matter of time before all the pieces fell into place.

The story he had spun was mostly true. Arnau Leport, aka The Catalan, was indeed a mercenary. A hit-man for hire, who played for whichever side paid the most in hard currency. He was a skilled operator, and one of the elite of his craft.

But for Mark Vashtan, Leport was not just a rogue operative. He was the man who had almost single-handedly destroyed his career.

It was back during the days when 'extraordinary rendition' had been a big part of the CIA playbook. These were operations that were never technically complicated, but always required supreme precision and tight coordination. Vashtan had been the point man in more than one of these operations, where a suspected terrorist would be plucked unwittingly off the street and whisked away to a place that didn't officially exist for a round of "spirited" interrogations.

In short, it was kidnapping.

Morally questionable, perhaps, but it was still a tactic that was astonishingly effective. And so it continued. Until a strange thing started happening. Intended targets would drop dead just as they were about to be snatched up. It was always done cleanly, almost elegantly - a sniper's bullet through the throat, or a subtle shove into oncoming traffic. And a rich source of prime intelligence would be lost in an instant.

It was always Leport, that much they knew, but the '*how*' and, most importantly, the '*why*' had always remained a mystery.

But for these questions the Professor would not provide Mark Vashtan with an answer.

Instead, he would spin another story. This one also true. Arnau Leport did not play for just one side. In North Africa, a pair of enterprising agency operatives had found another way to make use of the Catalan's talents. In a series of off-book (i.e. illegal) operations, the Catalan was employed to track down African paramilitary units that roamed the ungovernable areas of that continent, kidnapping European tourists for ransom. Leport's job was to wait for the ransom to be paid, then find the kidnappers (with the help of intelligence provided by his new agency friends) and then swiftly kill them. The Catalan's fee was always 30% of the appropriated ransom, with the rest returned to the agency men who had surreptitiously contracted him. The scheme worked well, for a time, before other, more lucrative options appeared on the horizon.

And as the Catalan's expertise and acumen grew, his unparalleled skill at targeted executions soon became a well-known (and valuable) asset in the secret war now played out across the globe.

By the time the Professor had finished telling Vashtan about the agency's connection to Leport's rise, he could see the young man was practically boiling with anger. "Son-of-a- bitch!" Vashtan had spouted, his face practically purple, rage clouding his ability to see the bigger picture. He was fixated. "Who? Who were they? I need to know names!"

Predictable.

The professor knew that all of his failed missions had taken a toll on Vashtan, both professionally and personally. And that he would do *anything* to find those he thought responsible.

He had pleaded with Vashtan to act judiciously, to proceed with caution. But he knew what Vashtan's response would be even before Vashtan did.

"Who?!" Vashtan insisted.

The professor strategically gave in...

"I cannot say for sure, but rumour has it there were two partners working out of Casablanca. Hernandez and Strickland, I believe. They were exonerated, officially of course, but again, who is to say for sure..."

It was at that point that Vashtan had hastily abandoned his mostly-full glass of Chianti, making some transparently vague excuse about train times, and brusquely headed for the gate. He had to get back to Rome, to make calls, to get to the bottom of things. Was it just Strickland and Hernandez, or had the agency itself been protecting Leport all this time? He smelled a coverup. The Professor had given him just enough to finally start digging for answers.

But the Professor had not told him everything.

Outside, the clouds had begun to part and a single ray of sunshine filtered through the smoked glass window, dancing on the cube-shaped, cherry red Brionvega antique radio on the Professor's desk. He fiddled with the dials, trying to find a suitable station, soothed by the blinking red analog nodes on the control panel, a respite from the suffocatingly digital world on the outside. He had paused for a moment on a RAI news update, when the beige rotary phone hanging on the wall beside him rang loudly.

"*Pronto*"

A rough sounding, accented voice responded through the heavy static on the other end of the line.

"It is done. I have the package and am ready for your instructions, *sis plau*..."

"Very well," the Professor responded languidly. "Vashtan has been set in motion. Allow him to do the work, then, you may make your move."

"So be it."

The Professor hung up the phone and returned to his radio. Scanning through the broadcasts, he settled on a 1970s classic from Franco Califano and turned up the volume.

Eyes squinting in the newly bright sun, a wry grin crossed his lined face as he thought how pleasing it was to be back in the game. It was the only thing that he knew. It was the only thing that he loved.

Califano crooned from the single speaker on the old Brionvega: "Tutto il resto e' noiaaaaaaaa..."

Everything else is boring.

The Professor could not have agreed more.

TALLIN, ESTONIA

B altic station chief John Vincent was pissed-off. It was 11:30am and the morning's cable intercepts from the rented tramp-steamer cruising the icy waters off the Estonian coast still hadn't been filed and summarised. The dispatch to Washington was supposed to go out in twenty minutes, and it wasn't in the station chief's job description to be reading raw Intel.

"Damnit, where the hell is Angel Hernandez? His ass is mine when I get a hold of that bastard. Natalie!......Damnit, NATALIE! Where the fuck is Hernandez!?"

Natalie Chalmers was the agency delegated per-
sonal assistant for Chief Vincent. Twenty-nine
years old and counting, the University of Virginia
educated Richmond native wasn't your everyday
secretary. Drafted into a highly competitive and
super-secret branch of the Directorate of Operations just after graduation, the dark haired and
athletic Ms. Chalmers was field-certified and had
spent a rotation as an active SpecOps Officer in
South America before an ill-advised affair with an
embassy employed national got her sent back to
Washington and then relocated to this frigid assignment. It was a slap in the face for Natalie, and
a definite setback for her career ambitions. But at
least they let her out in the field again and hadn't
downgraded her security clearance. Cleaning up
after Vincent's mess was just a brief stop before
she was back on track. It was just a matter of staying out of trouble – no small task for a pretty girl
who the boss had his eye on. It was a fine line.

"Mr. Vincent. I haven't seen Officer Hernandez
since last Friday. I'll check with the duty manager
to see where he is."

"Good, get on it. If Hernandez isn't back here by
noon, he'll be taking orders from the clerical staff
back on the beltway."

Natalie didn't like chasing down wayward officers
who were doing the work she could do with her
eyes closed, but that was life at the moment. The

duty officer checked the books and confirmed the worst.

"Officer Hernandez checked out of the office on Friday. Bereavement flight, I think. From our records he took a flight on Finn Air to Helsinki, then connected to Brussels before flying back to Atlanta. That's where our records have him."

"Atlanta...who died?"

The duty officer stared back blankly.

"You said it was a bereavement flight."

"I don't know, Ms. Chalmers – Hernandez didn't give many details."

"Listen, could you do me a favour and get me his contact number...better yet, try and get him on the horn for me ASAP. We have an issue here that needs to be resolved."

Natalie sat back down at her desk and let out a slightly dispirited sigh as she reflected on just how boring and routine her life had become.

"Just a matter of time," she reminded herself. "Just a matter of time."

20 minutes later and the duty officer didn't have good news.

"We can't get in contact with Hernandez, Ms. Chalmers. I called the domestic staff in Atlanta and they tell me he hasn't checked in with them. What should I do, Ma'am?"

"Check the FAA records...then forget about it."

We've got more important things to do.

Natalie went back to her quotidian schedule of regular paper-shuffling and soon enough she too forgot about Angel Hernandez.

Then she got an interesting call from an old friend.

Natalie had met Mark Vashtan a few years ago at a terrifically boring conference on human smuggling down in Marseille. Being of a similar mind as to the merits of the nasally-sounding speaker who droned on incessantly in his irritatingly French-accented English, the two had slipped out early and headed down to a little hole-in-the-wall restaurant in a shady neighbourhood by the port. That night they had bonded over a wonderful local Bouillabaisse, a classic hearty fish stew, and about 2 or 3 bottles (she couldn't remember which) of an excellent white Burgundy from near Macon. After dinner, and more than one Armagnac, one thing had led to another, and then...

Suffice it to say she wasn't disappointed to hear Mark's voice on the other end of the line.

It was strange to hear from him after all this time, but the favour he asked was even stranger. It turns out there was more than one person looking for

Angel Hernandez.

As she was pondering the coincidence, her desk phone rang again. It was the duty officer.

"Are you still interested in finding Angel Hernandez?"

Natalie smiled and shook her head, her wavy dark-brown hair just brushing the top lapels of her tailored Armani suit-jacket.

"Funny you should ask."

ROME, ITALY

Vashtan's apartment was in the Parioli neighbourhood, an elegant residential quarter in the north part of Rome. Just off the Viale dei Monte Parioli, the cube-shaped modernist complex sat partially hidden behind a row of thick bamboo hedges. His flat was on the top floor - a modified penthouse - and had reflective floor-to-ceiling windows on two sides, framing the curving street and the rows of Mercedes and Alfa Romeos parked haphazardly on the stone curb-side below.

Inside it was all clean lines and minimalist, a Murphy bed tucked neatly up into the wall, and a modern galley kitchen glistening in stainless steel spotlessness along one side. There was a two-seat black leather sofa facing a medium sized television and a sleek grey record player with an old Jobim bossa nova disc hiding under the scratched translucent cover. It was a quintessential bachelor pad, and Vashtan loved nothing more than slipping on his suede Bruno Magli loafers and sinking into his couch-seat, a Serie A soccer match and a glass of wine lulling him to sleep.

It was a big change from his first apartment in a family building far out along the Via Cassia. It was quieter here, but sometimes Vashtan missed the smell of simmering sauces and fresh bread wafting through the hallways of his old place, some hidden grandma working culinary magic from a long forgotten age. But Vashtan didn't have a family, and the stilted silence of Parioli suited his lifestyle better than the screaming children and arguing spouses of his previous residence. So here he was, tucked into a cocoon of peaceful sterility, enjoying as best he could the tranquility of his surroundings.

But today, nothing in his life was tranquil.

He had gotten off the phone with Natalie just a handful of hours ago and knew what needed to be done. And it had to be done fast.

His leather tote bag was half-filled, sitting on the polished wooden floor, various and sundry items spilling out everywhere. He was trying to pack and had only 3 hours until his flight from Fiumicino to Miami, and then on to Belize. He was not ready.

Complicating matters further was the fact that his old flame Natalie had insisted on accompanying him to track down Angel Hernandez. Vashtan had enough troubles at the moment, and the presence of Natalie would be an unwanted distraction. He could already see her slender legs and emerald green eyes and the way they sparkled when she smiled at him coyly from one side of her mouth. He was imagining how the sultry humid heat of the tropics would make her clothes cling seductively to her long, lithe body, a little puddle of perspiration collecting in the small of her back.

'Damnit,' he thought to himself. 'Definitely a distraction,' as he tried his best to put her out of his mind.

It was an exercise in futility. 'Damnit' he thought again.

Vashtan felt that familiar itch as he saw the open bottle of Jack Daniels sitting invitingly on the counter, the combination of stress and desire making his mouth water.

Just as he reached to pour himself a suitably strong cocktail, the intercom from the front door buzzed angrily. His taxi was already here to pick him up.

'Damnit.'

BELIZE CITY, BELIZE

Angel Hernandez stood in the corner of his hotel room and stared out over the choppy blue waters of the Caribbean sea. It had been two days since the Agency had tracked him down, and he knew that his time as a free man was running short. He took a long pull from the bottle of the heavy, dark Demerara rum that he held loosely in his right hand and savoured the rich sticky molasses taste - sloshing it around slowly in his mouth and feeling a connection with all the sailors, pirates, louts, and losers who had been drinking the same magic sugarcane potion for centuries long past. It was a classic salve for wounds both mortal and psychic, but it wasn't doing Angel Hernandez any good.

He knew that what was in store for him would not be pleasant. He knew this was true. But he'd had no choice. They had cornered him and there was nothing that he could do. At least that's what he kept repeating to himself between gulps of rum and chain-smoked cigarettes. There was nothing that he could do.

He would tell Vashtan what he wanted to know. Not the whole story, of course. That would be sui-cide - there was no way Vashtan could protect him from THEM, especially since his life-insurance policy expired when the Catalan recovered the package. But he would tell Vashtan just enough to get himself sent to some military prison some-where in the Carolinas where his daughter could at least come and see him at Christmas. It seemed like a fair deal.

And at least he had given Pete Strickland a head start.

Hernandez ambled back to the big, beige armchair facing the cable television and turned up the vol-ume. There was an NFL football game on, and the Raiders were playing...poorly. He had already or-dered a club sandwich and two beers from room service, and was hoping the combination might do the trick where the rum had failed. Plus, he was hungry.

After a Raiders fumble and some colourful cursing from Hernandez, there was a knock at the door.

'Finally,' Angel thought as he grabbed a generous twenty dollar tip from a messy stack of bills on the bedside table, 'I'm fucking starving.'

But there was no food waiting for him.

When Vashtan and Natalie arrived at the Radisson about 20 minutes later, they found Hernandez's door slightly ajar - the sound of ruffling curtains and the ocean murmuring in the background. Not a good sign.

Stepping cautiously inside, they saw Angel's body spread-eagled on the floor, the side of his skull crushed in, rivulets of blood streaking his face and pooling in a dark purplish mess on the grungy stained carpet.

Vashtan walked over and knelt down next to the seemingly lifeless body and checked for breathing, a pulse, anything. As he touched the side of Angel's neck, the body convulsed violently forward, Hernandez choking on the crimson blood bubbling up from somewhere deep inside. He gasped and choked again, this time a pinkish foam oozing from his lips like some horror show of molecular gastronomy, and then slumped back down on the floor.

Vashtan grabbed him hard around the shoulders. "Who did this to you?! Where's Pete Strickland?"

Hernandez's eyes were shaded in black and swollen nearly shut, his breathing barely a raspy murmur, as he struggled to force a sound from his broken diaphragm.

"Elday...elday..." the life slowly draining from him, expiring with each forced gurgle.

Vashtan shook him again, this time harder.

"C'mon buddy, I need you alive! Tell me something! Who?!"

Angel's cratered head slumped to one side as he whispered a final, barely audible syllable.

"Effffayyyy..."

Natalie was still standing in the narrow, short foyer by the door, one foot inside the bathroom, a 9mm Beretta drawn scanning the background. She nodded her head slightly upward at Vashtan:

"Is he alive?"

Vashtan didn't respond at first, then stood up slowly and walked silently past Natalie out to the sidewalk beyond the door, and lit a cigarette.

"He's dead."

FLORES, GUATEMALA

V ashtan lay naked on the old rattan-frame bed, smoking yet another filtered Camel cigarette, staring up at the metal ceiling fan in its lurching gyrations. The dull, ratty white sheets were soaked in sweat, and the sweet flowery aroma of the local detergent filled the room. Vashtan took another drag from his cigarette and enjoyed the feeling of the cool lake-side air caressing his upper body. He was starting to sober up, so he walked over to the little table by the window and made himself another drink. Three rocks, two fingers, and a splash. Sinatra style.

He stood there quietly, looking out at the skinny little isthmus that stretched across this narrow part of Lago Peten Itza, connecting the tiny island of Flores to the grungy mainland and new international airport on the other side. The gateway to the Maya - or so they called it. For Vashtan it had simply been the gateway to hell.

He had spent a few days drinking himself senseless in Belize, taking up his old pack-a-day smoking habit. The one he had given up three years ago. He had taken the Hernandez thing hard. Harder than even he could have expected. After all, he didn't know Hernandez, much less like him. He was a goddamn traitor, and probably deserved to die anyway. But it was the old feeling of helplessness that came back to hit him in the gut. That sucker punch that leaves you winded and angry. It was the same as before, the closer you came to an answer the more likely it was to slip away. It was infuriating. Maddening even. And so Vashtan had reached for the bottle - - and hadn't yet put it down.

Natalie had watched him as he spiralled quietly into a deep, dark alcoholic cloud. She didn't say anything, instead spending the time tracking Hernandez and Strickland's Caribbean movements. She went out to San Pedro, made famous by Madonna's 'La Isla Bonita,' and had dragged Vashtan in his stupor to a rough reggae bar built into a treehouse in Caye Caulker where Vashtan was pretty sure he had smoked a joint with a rasta guy while listening to Concrete Jungle. In any case, it was all a haze.

Natalie was a good spy, a great spy actually, thought Vashtan. Thorough and diligent, but flexible enough to get the job done in the most ambiguous of circumstances. She was street-smart too, and had an instinctive ability to get answers from even the most reluctant of sources. In short, she was a natural.

So he wasn't surprised when she managed to track down Pete Strickland's last move - a bus ride out to the Guatemalan jungle.

"Nice work Chalmers," he remembered telling her, "couldn't have done better myself." He had said it ironically, angrily even. But Natalie had responded only gently and without any malice, using his first name.

"Mark, you're not well" she had told him.

He knew that already, but more importantly, he was glad that someone else knew it too - and without judgment. It was that little knowing that gave him some solace, and just a little bit of rope to hold on to his sanity.

Vashtan came back from his quiet reverie and finished his drink in a long gulp. He was about to pour himself another when the door to the bathroom opened, white steam billowing from the door as Natalie got out of the shower, nude and still wet, a towel turbaned snugly around her head. She was facing away from him, floating there, seemingly suspended as she wiped away a strip of condensation from the heavily fogged mirror with a delicate swipe of her hand, and only then, through the already misting reflection, did she see Vashtan staring at her.

Sashaying seductively out into the small room, still dripping from the too-hot shower, she smiled at him in that way she knew always worked.

"Come back to bed..."

GUATEMALA, THE JUNGLE

L eport squeezed the little man's neck, pressing his thumb hard into the carotid artery, staring into those beady, panicked eyes until he heard the telltale gurgle that meant the struggle was over. The man had told him nothing. To be more precise, the now-dead man had told him nothing.

Leport was growing restless. He had followed the Professor's orders, letting Vashtan do the work, drawing out Angel Hernandez. It had worked, as it usually did, and Leport had taken a special pleasure in smashing in that arrogant man's moustachioed face. Hernandez was a gasbag, a paper-pushing phoney who was only out for himself. Leport thought it would be easy to beat the information out of him, thought he'd crack after the first few broken ribs. But Hernandez hadn't said a word about Strickland, or maybe he just didn't know. Either way, he had to give the man some grudging respect. I guess friendship goes a long way.

Without any useful information from Angel Hernandez, Leport had been stuck shadowing Vashtan and the girl. Well actually just the girl, truth be told. But their trail seemed to have gone cold on them, and they'd now been holed up out here in the jungle for days.

They weren't getting any closer to Peter Strickland.

Strickland had been savvy to come out here. Blending in with the nonstop tourist flows heading out to the national park at Tikal. Just another white face in a crowd of bulky, middle age, faux-adventure seekers. Very savvy indeed.

With no forward movement, Leport had become insufferably bored. There was nothing to do except wait, drinking beers and eating the local chicken, grilled over big metal charcoal-filled drums from the innumerable roadside vendors. He was not interested in the dead-eyed whores or the listless, slow-moving frumpy tourists shopping for bargains. He was interested in only one thing - finding Strickland.

So he had started actively hunting on his own. The skinny customs agent from the airport was just one of a few poor souls that he had dragooned and then murdered out here among the hidden Mayan ruins. But still he had gotten no leads. Only a succession of ignorant corpses.

The Professor would not be pleased with him - thought Leport - making his own moves out here in the jungle. He could imagine the old man chastising him now - "always swim sideways with the current, no wasted movements - thrashing angrily is how people die."

It was just one of a multitude of aphorisms that the Professor had always used to express his preferred modus operandi.

Wait in the shadows, use the momentum of your adversaries, strategic jiu jitsu.

Leport had listened for almost twenty years now, and he knew that the Professor was right. He was a wise man, after all, surviving in the game all these years, until a single mistake had sidelined them both five years ago. But now Leport was restless. Vashtan and the girl were getting nowhere. He wanted to kill again, to keep killing until he slaughtered his way to Strickland.

But the Professor's voice in his head was still strong: "Trust in the oblique angles, the answer will come..."

And so Leport went back into town. He would order a bottle of ice-cold Gallo beer, stare emptily through gold-rimmed aviator sunglasses at yet another of the black rooster labels, and wait.

PARIS, FRANCE

N atalie sat outside at one of the many small, round metal tables lining the sidewalk on a cobbled and shady side-street near the Place Pigalle, drinking a coffee and reading the International Herald Tribune, or whatever it was they called the American paper these days. Guatemala had been a dead end, and so she had decided to take some time off and bring Vashtan here to the City of Light. He couldn't go back to Rome. Not like this. He was sick, drinking too much, and wouldn't function in an office.

They had taken a studio flat up near Montmartre,

a tiny place with a cramped little bathroom and a double-burner hotplate for a kitchen. The walls were painted a dark burgundy, and the thick red curtains blocked the light from the tall double window facing the street. It felt like a bordello. But in the morning, with the drapes pulled back and the window open, the cool air brought with it the aroma of fresh baked bread and croissants, coffee, and distant cigarette smoke, all mixing in a continental melange of sensations, floating together with the tiny, glistening dust particles dancing in the streaming morning sunlight.

Like most days, Vashtan was sleeping late, so Natalie was alone. She had already eaten breakfast, and, always preferring savoury to sweet, had asked for a Croque Madame in her best French imitation. She had taken up smoking since Belize, and had a lit cigarette smouldering in a marble ashtray on the table, delicate wasps of smoke sneaking up through the pages of her newspaper before disappearing into the light blue sky of autumnal Paris. Natalie took a drag of the smoke, and laughed to herself thinking of how Mark choked every time he tried to smoke one of HER cigarettes. Filters were for pussies anyway, she thought, flicking the end of the bright-yellow, unfiltered Gitanes with her thumb, depositing a thin grey ash on the sidewalk.

She was reading a long exposé on a new corruption scandal sweeping the halls of Brussels, but couldn't keep her mind off Guatemala. Vashtan had told her about Leport, about the years of futility he had spent chasing the Catalan. About the blown operations, dead informants, and unanswered questions. She was intrigued, and finally stimulated after pushing papers for far too long in Tallinn. Vashtan was onto something, enigmatic for sure, but it was something. She had wanted to help him so badly down there in Belize. She had done her best, but had still come up short. It nagged at her. What had she missed? What else could she have done?

But the question that bothered her the most was the central one - where the hell was Peter Strickland?

Natalie knew for sure that he had taken that bus out of Belize City. She had found traces of him in San Ignacio, heard whisperings of his passing in Melchor, and followed his scent all the way to Flores. But from there the trail went dead cold. Like he had never been there at all.

'Well, what did she expect?' She thought to herself. Strickland wasn't an amateur after all, and if he was in as deep as Vashtan thought he was, well, he must have had some contingency plans in place. She definitely would, if she were in his shoes.

But she wasn't in his shoes, damnit, and kept replaying the events of those days over and over in her head. Maybe she had missed something? A clue unnoticed, a lead not pursued. But there was nothing. Ever since Hernandez bit the dust and Vashtan went on his bender, it had just been a wild goose chase.

If only they had gotten there in time to talk to Hernandez. He knew something, that much she was sure of. But his brains were already splayed all over the floor of the Radisson when they arrived, and Vashtan said he could only muster some kind of monosyllabic drooling while drowning in his own blood. Complete nonsense he had said.

She took another long drag on her cigarette, inhaling deeply, and blew the smoke skywards, sighing to herself. "Nonsense."

A little black and white spotted tabby cat had lazily crept up under her table and then jumped gracefully into her lap, purring loudly. She was happy for the company, and the distraction, and stroked the feline's arching back, the cigarette in her right hand dangling just below the seat of her chair. A tall moustachioed waiter walked by carrying a tray of empty glasses. He stopped abruptly beside her table and said something in a heavily Parisian type of French, glowering at her condescendingly. But she just looked up at him indifferently, and continued to pet her newfound friend. The waiter said something again, pinching his eyebrows tight and gesturing at the cat with his stubby nose. But Natalie just shrugged her shoulders and smiled at him nonchalantly. She didn't understand-it sounded like nonsense to her anyway. The waiter turned and walked away, muttering more nonsense to himself.

Then it hit her. Nonsense. Of course!

She put the cat gently down on the sidewalk, stubbed out her cigarette and then bounded up the steep stone staircase, two steps at a time, towards Montmartre. It was time for Mark to wake up.

Moments later, at another table just steps away, a bearded man with close-cropped hair finished his cloudy watered-down *pastis* and paid his bill. Leaving the cafe, he slipped on a pair of gold-rimmed aviator sunglasses, zipped up his black leather jacket, and walked leisurely around the corner to a parallel street heading up the hill. Towards Montmartre.

ZIPOLITE, MEXICO

Swaying gently back and forth in the salt-encrusted woven nylon hammock that had been his bed for the past three nights, Pete Strickland stretched out his long legs and yawned. He looked out at the vast expanse of the Pacific Ocean, emerald green and then a deep, dark blue fading into the white dotted horizon, and thought how lucky he was to have made it this far.

A half-finished Indio beer dug into the course brown sand under his shoe-less feet, the wind whistling through the neck of the glass bottle. Tilting his head back, he listened to the rhythmic squeaking of the ropes that tied his hammock to a pair of thin wooden pylons underneath a corrugated metal rooftop. This was the cheapest place to sleep here on the beach in Zipolite. Only ten dollars a night to swing alongside twenty or so other drunk hippies. It wasn't bad. There were some sand flies that you had to get used to, and the occasional scorpion darting across the sand, but it was nothing a bottle of mezcal before bed couldn't cure.

It had been a long road here to the Pacific. One bus after another through Guatemala, across the border and through Chiapas, and then up to Oaxaca City. He had spent a pleasant night there, drinking thick hot chocolate and watching the vendors selling shiny, brightly coloured balloons in the zocalo, before taking a rickety micro-bus over the wild curving roads that led through the Sierra Nevada mountains and here to the Oaxacan coast of Mexico.

For weeks he had slept in bus depots, cheap hostels, and dilapidated motels. His beard had grown in, scraggly and unkempt, reddish-brown except for the strips of white hair under his chin and along one cheek. He was tired, and wanted a good shower and a comfortable bed. It had been too risky to stop until now. He knew they would be following his trail out of Belize. He had to move quickly, without attracting attention. Burrowing deep off the grid. It seemed like it just might have worked too. He had covered enough ground and made enough twists and turns to start to feel almost safe. But not safe enough.

He'd rough it out here for a few more days on Zipolite, watching and waiting, checking for signs of surveillance. His cash supply was still good, and he had a thin strip of gold bullion hidden in one of the hollowed out soles of his thick brown-leather Danner hiking boots. Just in case.

If all went well, in a few days he'd be up the coast, lounging in a plunge pool at Las Brisas, a piña colada in one hand, a cuban cigar in the other, gazing out over the red and orange sunset framing Acapulco Bay. Just a few more days, he thought.

Pete had been planning this for a long time. Ever since he and Hernandez had hired the Catalan back in Casablanca, he knew this day might come. They had made a great deal of money with Leport, more than enough to retire someplace warm. It had been a good gig. The ethics of the situation never seemed to bother Pete - after all, they hired Leport to kill bad guys. So what if there was some extra money in it for him and his partner. No one ever got rich by following the rules.

And so he played the game, and the money had flowed in. The bankers he found in Mexico were discrete, didn't ask any questions. Seemed they were used to this kind of thing. The treasure chest grew - a few off-shore trusts on the islands, but most importantly the vault in Mexico City. He kept a huge fortune there, fully liquid, just in case the shit hit the fan and he was *persona non grata*, a man on the run.

He always knew who he'd be running from. It wouldn't be his agency, the government, Interpol or the tax man. No, it would be the man who introduced him to the Catalan in the first place. An old man who had a curving scar on his cheekbone and walked with a cane. It was always going to be him.

The Professor didn't have any loyalties. Only interests. And for a good while their interests had aligned. Leport worked for them, but he belonged to the Professor. They always knew that. It was never a problem, and the Catalan had always coloured inside the lines they had drawn, while the Professor hid in the shadows.

And then came Europe. The Milan job. Rome. Lugano.

The Catalan started going off script. He was doing jobs with an agenda they couldn't understand. Seemingly at random. And so they couldn't be tied to him any longer. Not with all the heat.

They had tried to take Leport out with a hit in Malaga, but failed. And that's when the Professor came out from his lair. Their interests had diverged from his, but more than that he was angry. And in his anger he had made his only mistake.

For five years, Pete and Angel had used that mistake as an insurance policy to keep the Professor on the sidelines. Five years of quiet blackmail. The information they had in the package could shut the old man down. But it couldn't last forever. It was always going to go bad.

Pete sat partially upright in his red, green and yellow twisted hammock and watched a pair of nudists walk hand-in-hand down the long curving beach, a pair of flaccid white buttocks staring back at him...

"Yeah, it was always going to go bad."

He took a last sip of his now-warm beer and then walked up the uneven wooden walkway across the sand, to the little taqueria that served the best spit-roasted pork, pineapple, and cilantro tacos in town. He had two, and an ice-cold Pacifico, savouring every bite.

Pete looked down at his bare feet, dirty brown and calloused, his nails a bit too long, tufts of hair protruding from the knuckles of his big toes. He noticed for the first time the extent of his filthiness, and the sour smell emanating from his pit-stained shirt.

"Fuck it."

Tomorrow he would leave for Acapulco.

MONTMARTRE, PARIS

V ashtan turned over in bed and pulled the yellowing sheets over his head, trying to hide from the blaze of sunlight pouring in through the window across the tiny room. He lay there for a few moments with his eyes closed, the onset of a hangover lurking out there in the world of the living. He tried to sleep, to delay the inevitable, but it was pointless. The throbbing pain in his head was only getting worse, slowly pushing its way to the front of his consciousness, bringing with it a hint of nausea and self-loathing.

"Jesus," he thought out loud, pulling a stray pillow tight over his eyes. "Why does she always have to open the goddamn curtains."

He was thirsty and dehydrated, and desperate to wash the phlegmy ashtray paste from the roof of his mouth. Unable to muster the strength to take the few steps to the bathroom sink, he reached for the pack of camels on the nightstand instead. At least there was nicotine. He lit his first cigarette of the day, sitting up in the rickety old futon, his back against the exposed brick wall. He took a slow, deep drag and looked out the window, trying to think of nothing at all.

About halfway through cigarette number three, Vashtan heard the sound of jingling keys in the doorway outside.

Natalie was back, a tall cup of Parisian Kusmi tea in one hand, trailing vapour like a Victorian steam train.

"Good, you're awake" she said, handing Vashtan the steeping beverage. "We need to talk. I think I've got something."

Vashtan grimaced. "Number one, I'm not awake" he said, taking the steaming cup with both hands. "Number two, does this have bourbon in it?"

Natalie smiled out of the corner of her mouth - "Not yet" - she said, and pretended not to notice as Vashtan stumbled over to the little table under the window where they kept the bottles.

"Mark, we need to talk about Belize City."

"Jesus Christ."

"Come on Mark, I know we've been over this before but it's important."

"We're out of bourbon."

"For fuck's sake, be serious!"

"I am serious," he said, the momentary panic leaving his face as he noticed a half-filled bottle of artisanal cognac sitting on the windowsill. The one he had bought in that gypsy jazz joint out by the flea market near the Porte de Clignancourt. 'This will have to do' he thought, emptying a long pour into his breakfast tea. "We really need more booze."

"Damnit Mark, try to help me out here" pleaded Natalie with just a touch of desperation. "You can't keep going on like this."

Vashtan looked up at her, his bloodshot eyes suddenly very sad, betraying the pain that was eating him alive.

"You're right. I know you're right. But there's nothing there. I don't have any answers." Vashtan stared down at the stained red carpet, scrunching his toes into the fraying fibres. The helplessness was washing over him again, like some slowly creeping malaise, pushing him to the precipice of madness. "I don't have any answers at all."

Natalie walked over and took his hand gently in hers. "Maybe you do and you just don't know it."

Vashtan sat down in the chair by the table, burying his head in his hands.

"Why are you torturing me Natalie? I already gave you everything I've got."

"Just wait. Please. Hernandez--before he died. He said something, right?"

"No. He didn't. Like I told you, it was nonsense."

"How do you know it was nonsense?"

"Because I understand the goddamn English language, Natalie. Jesus Christ, it was fucking gobbledy-gook. Ellday, ellday, effay...some shit like that...who knows, he was spitting up blood, dying for fuck's sake. Trust me, it's a dead end."

"What did you ask him?"

"Come on, just let it go!"

"Indulge me. What did you ask?"

"I asked him who bashed his fucking brains out."

"Is that all?"

"Yeah, that's it." Vashtan thought back for a second, fighting through the mind-numbing pain in his temples..."and then I asked him where Strickland was."

Natalie mouthed the words over and over, her brain processing...ellday, ellday...ellday, ellday... effay. Effay. Ellday. Effay. ELLDAY. EFFAY.

"That's not nonsense" Natalie said, the smile creeping back across her lips. "It's Spanish."

Vashtan suddenly realised it too. "Angel Hernandez, you son of a bitch."

El D.F.

The *Distrito Federal*.

Peter Strickland was heading for Mexico City.

FLORENCE, ITALY

A dense grey mist hung low in the sky, obscuring the red tiled rooftops of down-town Florence. After days of the Tuscan indian summer, known as the *ottobrata*, the rain had returned, pushing over the Appenine ridge to the east, and trapping a cold, damp blanket over the manicured Chianti countryside. It was the Professor's favourite time of the year - the time for roasted chestnuts and *novello* wine, for bright green olive oil fresh from the *frantoio*, and grilled saltless bread topped with sausage and velvety soft *stracchino* cheese. It was harvest time.

Unfortunately for the Professor, he had not been

able to fully reap the rewards of the seeds he himself had planted just a few short weeks ago. Yes, Hernandez was dead - but the trail for Strickland had died along with him. It was all taking too long, and the Professor knew why.

It was his miscalculation, to be sure, but how could he possibly have foreseen the extent of Vashtan's meltdown? Of course, the young man had been perched on the edge of an emotional precipice, that much he knew - and had counted on. It had taken only a slight nudge to send him spiralling toward Hernandez, just as predicted. But Belize had sent him into a violent tailspin - a colossal funk which had threatened to derail all of the Professor's well laid plains.

Thank god there was the girl. At first the Professor had been concerned that her presence might have put the brakes on the impulsive proclivities of Vashtan, potentially adding a layer of complexity to the predictability of a lone operator. But Vashtan had nosedived, and it was the girl who had taken up the mantle of chief detective in the desperate search for Strickland that the Professor had been sure would ensue.

Even so, the chessboard had not moved for days. Vashtan and the girl were still holed up in Paris, evidently more concerned with the amorous aspects of the game of life. The Professor was perturbed. Their relationship threatened to escalate from an annoying subtext to a real impediment to his goals. He needed them to push forward. Finding Strickland was on his critical path. He could not continue until the man had been eliminated. And time was running out.

Logic told the Professor that Vashtan and the girl would eventually be driven to resume the hunt, the human brain almost preternaturally opposed to unanswered questions. But when? The Professor was anxious, but not nervous. He had learned long ago to implicitly trust the quasi-predictable machinations of human nature.

That hint of anxiety though was immeasurably pleasing to the Professor. It meant that the game was worth playing, even if he was fairly secure in the knowledge that the eventual outcome would be to his favour. Still, he relished the slight tingle on the backs of his arms when he calculated the uncertainty of the next move.

As the Professor silently played out the scenarios in his mind, assigning probabilities and gauging impacts of various moves and countermoves, the phone for which there was only one caller rang unexpectedly.

The Professor answered, listened silently and then hung up without saying a word.

Finally, movement.

Vashtan and the girl had left their love nest in

Paris and boarded a flight for Rome. In two hours they would be in the Eternal City.

The Professor sighed, and poured himself a small glass of the slightly effervescent *novello* wine. He took a sip and pondered the rearranged pieces on his mental chessboard, one step closer to check-mate.

ACAPULCO, MEXICO

L as Brisas sits on the side of a steep hill overlooking the curving expanse of Acapulco Bay. Once the preferred retreat of the Hollywood jet-set, the collection of quaint cabanas now exuded a lush type of faded charm that made it a haven for those whose ideas of romance included a heavy dose of nostalgia with their afternoon cocktails and wood-slatted verandas. It was the perfect place for Pete Strickland to get just a taste of his soon-to-be luxurious life as a wealthy fugitive.

Sitting there in the dreamy glow of late-afternoon Acapulco, pitcher of hibiscus infused margarita on the breakfast table and a surprisingly smooth, yet richly flavoured Romeo y Julieta Numero Dos cigar in his hand, Pete was sure he could get used to this.

Upon arrival here in this formerly exotic resort town, now ravaged by years of drug wars and largely forgotten by the old North American clientele, Pete had begun to shrug off his weeks-long existence as a grubby, cash-starved backpacker. In this town, money talked, and gold talked even louder. He had ripped up his old hiking boots and traded in his stash of beaten-down bullion for a few good Zegna suits, 2 pairs of black leather lace-ups, a good old-fashioned shave, and a grade-A falsified Uruguayan passport which he had used when he checked into suite 22 at Las Brisas. So far, so good. He even had a little left over for some much needed spa treatments at the off-site beach club carved into the rocks down by the bay.

Pete leaned back into the soft beige pillows of the huge egg- shaped rattan chair and took another drag of the chunky cigar, now half burned. 'This is the life' - he thought to himself, a warm breeze flirting with the tails of his white button down shirt. 'To bad we gotta get this over with.'

He knew it was just an interlude - that the hard part was still to come. Mexico City was going to be delicate. Well, more than delicate, it was going to be dangerous. If anyone were going to find him now, it would be there in that teeming metropolis. It would be there, because, simply put, that's were the money was.

He had made it out of the first stages of his flight - the mad dash, the rush for the border, the serpentine escape to the Mexican hinterland. He had needed guile for that part, and a certain bit of cunning too. But this next act was going to require significantly more finesse.

Mexico City itself was not the problem. It was big enough to blend into easily, and had enough shady nooks and crannies to hide for a lifetime. But the move for the vault, his precious vault, would require him to be perfectly exposed. That moment, above everything else, would surely be the proverbial 'moment of truth.'

There was still planning to be done, even though he and his bankers had already established a rather elaborate protocol for just such an occasion. Still, nothing and no one could be trusted - he needed safeguards, and back-up options - mental assurances to himself that he had eliminated as much risk as humanly possible.

In two days he'd leave Acapulco and begin the tedious process of surveilling the upscale Polanco neighbourhood of Mexico City. It was there, tucked discreetly behind the JW Marriott hotel, were the small private bank that held his treasure was located. Hence the fancy business suits and slickly polished shoes. Sitting there with a cup of Starbucks, hiding behind a financial newspaper and the mirror-lensed Chanel sunglasses he had bought at the Las Brisas boutique, Pete would fit right in with all the other douchebags.

But for now, he'd slouch deep into his chair and enjoy the full pageantry of an Acapulco sunset, coloured sailboats bobbing in the bay, city lights reflecting in the calm blue water.

Maybe tomorrow he'd head to the old silver-mining town of Tasco, have a few tequilas and relax for one more day. Anyway, he knew a great place there for *enchiladas verdes*. And that, he thought, would be just too good to pass up.

PARIS, FRANCE

Arnau Leport sat upright in the simple metal chair placed squarely in the middle of the spartan room, his eyes closed tight against the midday sun pouring in through the partially open window. His breathing was smooth and steady, a now unconscious rhythm learned many years ago that took him to a faraway place of calm emptiness. And even though his black boots were placed firmly on the tiled floor of that Paris apartment, Leport was not there, instead drifting somewhere on the edge of time and space. He continued his breathing, silently in through his nose, then an audible rush of fully deoxygenated air exhaled through an open mouth. Slowly at first, then faster and faster into a hissing crescendo.

When he had finished his exercises, Leport opened his eyes and stoop up, surveying the barren studio flat that the Professor kept for him - one of many in the various European capitals where their business was silently conducted. It was better this way, more discreet, and anyway Leport had no patience for fawning hotel employees or the unwanted glances of curious fellow guests.

His duffel-shaped travel bag was placed next to the door, packed and ready for the flight to Rome, his black leather jacket hanging on the chrome hook just above. He was happy to leave. Happy to be one step closer to his and the Professor's full rehabilitation. It had been too long...much too long.

Glancing briefly out the window towards the Parisian cityscape, Leport thought back on his very first kill. It was here, in Paris, more than twenty years ago. Before the Professor found him, taught him, and gave him purpose. Back then he was still just a kid, innocent but for a dark simmering rage that he always knew was buried at the heart of his soul, hidden by an outward kindness that people saw in his gentle smile and mild manners. He was timid then, and just a little bit awkward, still clinging to the whimsical dreams of his youth. But just under the surface there was an anger that he could not explain, even to himself. From the outside looking in, it would have all seemed perfectly normal. Normal family, normal friends, a good student and a handsome young man. But from the inside...from the inside it had always been there, even if forcibly pushed down and hidden from the rest of the world.

Then, twenty years ago, it had suddenly bubbled to the surface. He was just an adventurous kid, traveling Europe on his own money, out of his beloved Catalonia for the very first time. It was his initial stop on a journey he had planned as a graduation present for himself. He would stay in hostels, go out to bars, meet girls...just a typical rite of passage for an adolescent looking out at the potential of a life yet to be lived.

He had gone out on his first night in Paris, one bar after another, in a blur of newfound friends, alcohol, and maybe a joint or two on narrow sidewalks and underneath raised train tracks away from the sterile heart of the tourist centre. He was young, and he was happy, and in his naiveté he had wandered off on his own further out into the outskirts of that beautiful and dangerous city.

That night, underneath a grubby overpass, in a graffiti-ridden concrete maze, his life would be forever altered. The gypsy kids had approached him as friends, two of them, laughing and joking, arms around his shoulders. They would take him to a fun place, very local, they had told him. Come along, come along they had said - over here, giggling and grinning, slapping him on the back - this way, my brother.

And then he had felt the pain in his side, saw the little knife clutched in the boy's hand, and the expressions that changed instantaneously to ugliness. Smiles now vicious sneers, demanding money. The other boy hit him in the face, knocking him backwards into a cinderblock wall. Two faces up close against his, spittle and menace raging against him as the two boys crowded him close, digging at his pockets, into his jeans.

He could remember that moment of panic when they had attacked him. But more clearly, he could remember that singular moment when the anger and violence that had always resided somewhere inside him suddenly rose up and took its place. That moment when his fist balled in anger, and a silent cry came up from deep in his soul giving a voice to his inner self.

He had beaten those boys to death that night. Pummelled them within an inch of their lives, then stood in silence over them, smiling, as he listened contentedly to their pathetic pleading before crushing their skulls with the boot of his shoe. He could remember the taste of the blood in his mouth, his scuffed knuckles, and the way their bodies had twitched at the end, the crimson stain spreading slowly across the concrete.

God, how good it had felt! The power that came with that release of unrestrained violence. Like a victorious gladiator, pulsing with bloody pride over his slain adversaries.

At that moment he knew his true self. His best self.

That Paris night was the first step on a journey that he would come to realise was preordained. A bloody destiny that would allow him to serve a purpose bigger than himself.

Leport opened his eyes again and returned to the present. He walked over to the door, put on his black leather jacket and grabbed his bag, before glancing one last time at the empty room behind him. It was time to leave Paris.

Destiny was calling.

ROME, ITALY

Vashtan stood in a somber type of silence on the pockmarked greyish-white travertine steps of the Aracoeli. Tall broccoli-topped umbrella pines dotted the piazza far below him, casting long shadows over the chaotic melee of automobiles careening wildly towards Piazza Venezia. In the pinkish dusky sky, hypnotic swarms of starlings danced in unison over the curving bends of the Tiber river, their cries echoing across the capital of modern Italy. In ancient times, augurs would divine the will of the gods by watching the flight of these migrating birds, their swirling patterns a secret language from on high.

But today, as day blended slowly into night, Mark Vashtan saw only chaos and fear.

Natalie was admiring the twin statues of Castor and Pollux standing guard over the Capitoline steps to the left, and even with her back turned toward him, Mark could sense she was smiling. She was happy to be in Rome. Happy to be with him. Happy to be working on something that mattered.

Vashtan had pulled strings and called in every favour to get Natalie temporarily transferred out of that ice-box in Tallinn and onto the Catalan case. It was his way of saying thank you, and even though it had been a big lift, he knew that he still owed her a great deal. Not necessarily an apology, but at the very least an explanation. After all, she had risked everything to keep him from unravelling after Belize and had somehow managed to pull him back from his private nightmare.

Now back in Rome, Vashtan had finally gotten himself under a modicum of control. The new lead in the search for Strickland had focused him, temporarily pushing back the curtain of his depression. But in spite of the good progress they had made in the case, he could still sense the old helplessness lurking inside him like a dormant virus, waiting until a moment of psychic weakness to attack.

With an uncomfortable warmth slowly spreading

across his chest, Mark took Natalie's hand tightly in his.

"Let's go. I want to show you something."

Together they headed southwest, past the ruins of the Theatre of Marcellus with its converted luxury apartments at the top, and down into the Jewish Ghetto - the smell of deep-fried artichokes wafting out from the smart trattorias lining the Via del Portico D'Ottavia. Fat waiters stood stiffly on the sidewalk, hands clasped behind their backs, while a few stray cats aimlessly roamed the street-side tables.

Turning sharply right after passing yet another Kosher taverna, Mark took Natalie down a narrow alley that led to the quaint Fontana delle Tartarughe, Bernini's delicate bronze turtles perched precariously on the edge of the fountain's upper basin. They grabbed a quick glass of wine at the little bar across the street and then continued on towards the Campo dei Fiori with its gathering masses, all eager for the night to officially begin.

They walked mostly in silence, smoking and dodging the growing tourist hordes and the already-drunk vagrants at the base of Giordano Bruno's brooding statue. A group of armed carabinieri stood watch at one end of the square, assault rifles slung low over their shoulders.

The cobbles of the long oval-shaped piazza were

still slick and wet from the now-shuttered flower stalls, a swirling reflection of street lights and neon swimming dizzily on the surface. It was beautiful and rough and just a little bit sad.

Trying to ignore the sour smell of cheap spilled wine and urine, they continued on, turning left just past a weathered old bar, its floor covered in crushed peanut shells and detritus, then headed through the Piazza Farnese and up to Via Giulia. Here they stopped, next to a rather plain church facade, unassuming but for the laureled skulls above the entrance and the strange adornments of skeletons and bones all quietly celebrating the inevitability of death.

"This is where it first went bad..."

Mark's voice slowly trailed off as he began the story of a tip about a dangerous jihadi fugitive and an operation that went inexplicably wrong. He wanted to tell her how his partner and best friend had been gunned-down here on these steps by an unseen sniper. How his buddy had told him beforehand that the operation was a waste of time, that the lead was thin at best, unreliable and dangerous at worst. How he hadn't listened.

But the words stuck in his mouth.

Natalie meanwhile was transfixed by the morbid church facade and stared dreamily at the decorated plaque of an alms box on the front wall. It was carved with a winged skeleton and read:

HODIE MIHI CRAS TIBI

Today me, then you

"What is this place?" she whispered, slightly taken aback.

Looking up above the doorway she noticed a tablet with a winged hourglass - 'time flies and then you're dead' she thought to herself, 'thanks for the reminder.'

"Seriously Mark, what is this place - and why are we here?"

Mark paused, momentarily reflecting on the sins of the past before answering.

"Well, this *place* is the home of an ancient confraternity that used to be responsible for burying the abandoned corpses of Rome. Nowadays it's more of a place for lost souls..." His voice trailed off.

"OK, that explains all the morbid allusions - but why exactly are we here?"

"This place haunts me Natalie..."

Just as he was about to begin his professional confession, a tiny old Peugeot rumbled past them on the cobblestone street, coughing black smoke from a dangling tailpipe. As the junky old car drove under the massive ivy-covered arch that spanned the breadth of Via Giulia, connecting the Palazzo Farnese with the river above, Vashtan noticed a figure partially reflected in the rearview mirror. A bearded man with close-cropped, dark hair.

A wave of panic gripped him as he grabbed Natalie in mid-sentence and then tore off sprinting a couple hundred paces down the street before ducking quickly up a small staircase and onto the main thoroughfare flanking the Tiber river.

"Come ON!" he shouted, dragging Natalie into a mad rush of oncoming traffic and then to the other side of the Lungotevere, before darting across the Ponte Sisto pedestrian bridge, crashing through the grungy buskers and gypsy bums hustling for cash.

"Get out of the way - FUORI!!!!" He screamed, tackling through one, then the other, pulling Natalie by the wrist behind him.

On the other side of the river, he continued his crazed flight deep into the winding nooks of Trastevere before finally stopping, out of breath and pouring with sweat, under a little fig tree by an unnamed and empty trattoria.

His heart was pounding, a terrible pain building in his chest.

"What the fuck was that?!!" Natalie shouted, tearing her wrist from his grasp.

Vashtan leaned over, trying to catch his breath in short spurts, the panic after the adrenaline starting to overwhelm him.

She slapped him hard across the face.

"Pull yourself together, GODDAMNIT! You could have fucking killed us just now!"

"I know...I know..." he was trying to breathe, "it's just that...I think I saw...no it can't be...I must be losing my mind..."

"Mark, take a deep breath and just tell me what the hell is going on. Do you think you can do that or am I going to have to hit you again?"

"No, no...I mean, yes...no...It was him - Leport - I saw him. Or at least I think I saw him. But why? It doesn't make any sense. Maybe my mind is just playing tricks on me. I mean, there, at THAT church. Maybe I just wanted to see him. NEEDED to see him."

The pain in his chest was getting worse, sweat pouring down his forehead. He closed his eyes, trying to regain a measure of control.

"I don't think you should be here, Natalie."

"Excuse me?"

"You need to leave. It's not safe. I can't be trusted. Get out now while you can."

Natalie took a step back and then gave him an ice-cold glare, hands on her hips in a pose of pure defiance. "The only way I'm leaving here is with you, on a plane, to Mexico. Case fucking closed."

Vashtan stared up at her through squinted eyes, still hunched over, and tried his best to look serious. He wanted to argue with her, insist it was the best thing for both of them. That if she really wanted to help she would just leave.

But he couldn't bring himself to lie. The simple truth was that he couldn't bear to have her on his conscience. And deep down, he knew that he needed her despite the growing danger. So he just stared at her, mute, his face frozen except for the nervous twitching in his left eye.

Natalie stepped in close to him, smiling sweetly out of the corner of her mouth. That sweet little smile that he could not resist.

Then she slapped him. Hard.

ROME, ITALY

Natalie sat silently in the backseat of the yellow numbered taxi as it made its way through the busy city centre and out towards Parioli. It was the night of the Roma-Lazio derby, and the taxi radio was tuned to the end of the game, the monotone announcer calling out the names of the players as they passed the ball among themselves, then rising into a high pitched squeal as a final chance was created..."*Totti, Totti, Totti...Gol! Gol! Goooooooool! di Francesco Totti!!!!*"

Natalie wasn't listening, instead staring blankly out at the passing monuments, her forehead pressed lightly up against the cold glass window, as the deep boom of celebratory grenades reverberated out from the bowels of the Stadio Olimpico in the distance.

"It sounds like Lebanon," Mark said softly.

It was the first time he had spoken to her since they had argued and the words came out aimlessly, as though they might not even be meant for her, just whispers to break through the empty space. His face, and his pride, still stung from before.

But he was not angry, instead drifting into a somber sort of resignation that was dangerously close to a place in his mind that he did not want to go.

Natalie was worried about him, but she did not respond. Tonight had only made a bad situation worse. It was no secret that Vashtan was haunted by the events of the past. That much she already knew, and had accepted. But now he was seeing ghosts, the spectre of that past threatening to completely obscure the present. If the phantoms continued then surely there was no way forward. She could manage the drinking and the inevitable mental self-flagellation that followed, but this... this was immeasurably worse.

She continued to stare out the window in pensive silence. Perhaps it was all too much to take, she thought, seriously doubting herself for the very first time. Maybe she should just give up the fight, pick up her marbles and go back to her desk in the Baltic. After all, she could not do this alone. Suddenly she felt very, very sad and let out a faint, barely audible sigh. Unconsciously she slumped her shoulders forward, her head tilting to one side.

Vashtan, alert to the slight change in posture, turned to her, his words strong and earnest this time, a purposefulness in his eyes she had not seen since before Belize: "I'm sorry" he said, looking directly at her.

Natalie reached out across the distance between them and put her hand on his knee.

"We've got an early flight tomorrow."

The radio crackled in the background with the continuing roar of the stadium crowd, and Mark Vashtan searched deep down for some reservoir of strength within him that had not yet been sucked dry.

A fresh-faced youth passed by them on a Vespa, punching his fist jubilantly into the crisp night air. "*Evvai!*" he yelled, "*FORZA!*"

The boy sped off into the distance, red and yellow scarf flapping in the wind as he expertly swerved through the impossibly tight traffic choking the Piazzale delle Belle Arti, one hand still raised in triumph.

"*Lazio merda!*" he shouted, other motorists laugh-

ing and honking their horns wildly in joint cele-
bration, "*FORZA ROMA! FORZA! FORZA!*"

Vashtan looked out at the mayhem building in
the streets, the hint of a smile starting to spread
slowly across his face.

"Forza," he said to himself. "Forza."

GARBATELLA, ROME, ITALY

On the other side of town, in the corner table of a dimly lit Hosteria tucked between a motor repair shop and a bookstore specialising in dirty magazines, Leport and the Professor sat face to face for the first time in many years. It was a bittersweet reunion.

"You believe he saw you?"

The Professor sat hunched over a plate of pan-fried pancreas, cutting into the unctuous organ meat, a delicacy of the 'quinto quarto' cuisine that was the speciality of the house. Along with heart, brain, spleen, thymus, and even salivary glands, the *quinto quarto* (the parts left over after the choice meat had been sold to the rich) had always been a favourite among connoisseurs of true *cucina povera* - poor man's cooking. The Professor fancied himself just that.

The Catalan, however, did not eat flesh, and picked absentmindedly at his plate of sautéed chicory and garlic.

"Impossible to say."

The Professor was not satisfied with the response, and put down his utensils, leaning them against the side of his shallow dish. He adjusted his wire-rimmed spectacles and fixed Leport with a dubious but not-quite-menacing stare.

"And if you were compelled to say?"

Leport looked back across the table. His eyes were perfectly calm, but there was just a hint of irritation in his clipped response.

"50-50."

The Professor exhaled loudly through his nose, and went back to his plate of calf glands. The Catalan had never been much of a strategist, he thought, more of a blunt instrument. But neither was he stupid, that much was certain, and the exaggerated brevity of his response hid an intuitive sense that was hard for Leport to explain in rational terms. It embarrassed him, this inability to express himself, so he took refuge in simplicity. It was a defence mechanism. The Professor knew this, and was careful not press too hard, lest he upset the Catalan's delicate sensibilities. Still, he needed more raw data to make a proper calculation on his own. So he tried a different approach.

"The girl was with him?" He asked, almost nonchalantly.

Leport hesitated for a moment, tapping the table with his little finger.

"Yes. I followed them to the church of the Morte. They stopped momentarily there, and then they ran."

"You pursued them?"

The Catalan shook his head - "I would not expose myself."

"No, you would not."

The Professor made a series of calculations in his head, and then continued with his query.

"Who was the first to flee?"

"He."

"And she followed?"

"He took her."

"Ahhhh..." the Professor sighed, "very good then."

A grey-haired waiter passed by, studiously avoiding them as he disappeared into the kitchen.

"What is the significance of this?" Leport asked, reaching for the ceramic carafe of wine in the middle of the table and refilling both glasses.

"You, my friend, are the one that haunts his waking dreams. An apparition. Nothing more than a shadow. She herself did not see you and so, like Saint Thomas, she will not believe. They will continue on their path. And you will continue to follow them."

"As you wish."

The Professor picked up his wineglass and reached out, clinking it with Leport's - "To the shadows then."

"To the shadows" replied the Catalan.

BRUSSELS, BELGIUM
Royal Museum of Fine Arts

The carved acacia-wood cane leaned slightly to one side, two neatly manicured hands resting on its smooth curved handle. A golden signet ring engraved with three tiny honeybees adorned the fourth proximal digit on the right hand of the cane's owner, who stood silently contemplating the multitude of faceless, dark-suited and hatted men cascading down the opaque watercolored painting hanging on the wall in front of him.

The Professor did not care for Belgian art in general, and the vulgarities of surrealism offended his patrician taste, but he secretly admired this impressionist-inspired version of Magritte's Golconda, its bucolic background reminding him of the Tuscan countryside near Vicchio, blue pastel mountains in the distance, the crook of a little stream passing through light green fields. But the Professor most identified with the faceless man in the overcoat, and slowly let himself slip away, until he too was floating there in suspended animation, a figure on a museum wall.

The calm and silent stillness was broken by the staccato click-clack echoes of approaching shoes, as a man in a finely tailored dark suit came to stand at the Professor's side. His hair was slicked-back with a heavy gel, and he jutted his hips forward over his feet spread shoulder-width apart - a confident posture that spoke to a lifetime of influence and power. He stood there quietly with his hands on his hips, his elbow nearly touching the Professor's side. They did not look at one another, instead staring directly forward at the Magritte.

After a few moments the dark-suited man spoke. "So you've returned?"

"Yes" replied the Professor, his single word heavy with meaning that perhaps only the dark-suited man could fully comprehend.

"That's good news. I was just lamenting to our friends how we've missed you. It's been much too long."

"Indeed. My sabbatical was not by choice, as you know, but I feel the winds have finally shifted."

"And it could not come at a better time, dear Professor. In your absence the masses have again been hypnotised by the gentle blanket of their false security."

"Yes, I agree. It has been quiet for too long."

"Yes, it has been quiet - and the people have become sheep. This disgustingly permissive welfare state of ours has blinded them with an over-abundance of empty liberties and coddled them with misguided policies that cater to their every whim. They think only of their short-term petty desires and know nothing of sacrifice. And as they preen in contentment, they slowly decay, lost in a maze of destructive narcissism. They are now nothing more than cattle, and in their docility they have allowed greed and corruption to flourish. All in the name of a lie they call liberalism."

The Professor nodded in agreement.

"Yes, I concur. The pendulum has once again swung too far to the left. Without realignment I am afraid this continent of ours will soon be nothing more than a festering wound. We must open their eyes."

"As always, dear Professor, you understand perfectly. Balance is required. And balance requires blood. We must be resolute in our actions. Only with calculated violence can we steer the ship of our society back on course. And as before, we must be the architects of that violence if we wish to manage the chaos that is to come."

"That is why I have returned."

"I'm glad to hear it. However, there is still the business of five years ago. May I assume it is finished?"

"Nearly. The Catalan is currently occupied with the task of eliminating the final obstacle in our path."

"Good. And his skills? They are still sharp? As you are aware, once we begin down this path there can be no mistakes. We cannot afford any missteps this time."

"I would not proceed otherwise."

"Very well then," the dark-suited man continued. "When the Catalan is ready we shall begin. Everything is already in place. I have two cells of radicals that are both primed for action. One group in Amsterdam and another in Madrid. As before, they are all Islamists, poorly-trained and ignorant. Less troublesome to manage than the politicals."

"That is optimal. If they are fully independent and compartmentalised it will be easier for the Catalan to sanitise once the operation is complete."

The dark-suited man nodded his head and then reached into his left breast pocket.

"Same place. Pelikanstrasse 37. First instalment in advance" he said, handing the Professor a small oddly-shaped silver key. "How long until the Catalan is ready?"

"As I mentioned before, he is currently preoccupied with another matter. But I will have a status report from him shortly."

"Is he close then?"

"Not geographically speaking, no...but it will not be long."

The Professor was purposefully vague in his response, but it was enough for the dark-suited man, who duly walked off, the click-clack echo of his shoes fading into the distance.

The Professor had a ticket on the Eurostar train to Paris, but he would now have to make other plans. There was the small matter of a lockbox in Zurich to attend to - and a million Euros in cold hard cash.

MEXICO CITY, MEXICO

T he pieces had all started to fall into place after Vashtan and Natalie made their big break back in Paris. Mexico City was definitely the key they had been missing, and finding Strickland's bank had been easy, once they knew where to look.

They had already made casual inquiries, and knew that Strickland had not yet withdrawn his stash. But he had definitely been there, the staff confirmed, and so it was only a matter of time before he showed his face again.

The bank employees had given them a good description: baseball cap, mirrored Chanel sunglasses, fancy black shoes. But they had been scoping the bank for two days now, and still there was no sign at all.

Then they saw him.

A lanky figure approaching in short rapid paces toward the bank entrance. Boston Red Sox baseball cap, mirrored Chanel sunglasses. It was him.

Natalie squeezed Vashtan's hand. They both knew that it was time to act, and instinctively got to their feet, pushing back the metal chairs of the street-side table as they quickly made their move.

Strickland was still approaching them, baseball hat pulled low, head down. He was only a few paces from the bank door. Then suddenly two bursts in rapid succession: pop-pop.

The body went instantly limp, like a marionette who's strings had suddenly snapped all at once. His knees slammed hard into the concrete sidewalk. For a moment he was completely motionless, frozen for just a split second in an upright prayer-like pose, before pitching forward, face-first, into the oncoming traffic.

A big lumbering dump-truck slammed on its brakes, tires squealing, but it was too late. The massive hulk of machinery slid forward uncontrollably, then made a slight, barely noticeable hop to one side, as it crushed the baseball-capped head under its terrible weight.

A woman who was passing by dropped her shopping bags and let out a high-pitched scream, her hands covering her mouth: "*Ayuda!!!!!*"

"Don't look" Vashtan said, forcibly turning Natalie away, "don't look."

Vashtan searched around, desperate for signs of the shooter. But there was nothing, just the faint cry of a police siren, far away in the distance.

But Vashtan did not need visual confirmation. Inside he already knew.

"LEPORT!" he screamed out, towards no one in particular. "LEPORT!"

His hands were shaking and he could feel that sickening feeling coming over him again...that black helpless rage that would swallow him whole.

Then he saw Natalie, her face white and frozen. Her mouth was slightly ajar and there was emptiness in her hazel and brown eyes. She was trembling uncontrollably, so he took her by the shoulders and sat her down gently in one of the metal café chairs.

He forced himself to recompose, straining to push away the building storm-cloud in his mind. Then he walked over to inspect the carnage.

Pete's body was a bloody pulp, completely unrecognisable. The force of the impact had knocked his shoes completely off his feet - a pair of scuffed

Puma sneakers lying ten yards apart on the other side of the street. His arms and legs were splayed wide in a disjointed mishmash of limbs, one hand clenched shut, the end of a 500 peso bill peeking out from still-closed fingers.

"All that money in the bank and he died with thirty measly dollars in his hand. Pitiful."

With nothing left to be done, Pete lit a cigarette, and walked slowly back toward Natalie.

It had happened again.

Ten blocks away, in a dilapidated phone booth on the edge of the park, Arnau Leport made a long distance call.

"It is done," said the Catalan. Then he hung up.

That night Mark Vashtan and Natalie Chalmers got drunk, this time together. There was tequila. A lot of tequila. Starting with a full-bodied golden *reposado* and then moving on to some decently smooth white agave, they drank with an angry ravenous abandon.

By the time they got to bottle number three, they couldn't really taste much anymore. So they opted for the cheapest bottle of house tequila at a supremely touristy bar in Plaza Garibaldi. The mariachi bands were out in full force, clad in black suits and wild, oversized sombreros, gold-trimmed and intricately decorated. They serenaded the increasingly intoxicated patrons who gathered throughout the square, song and laughter rising up together with the cracking fireworks, filling the open space with a cacophony of drunken jubilation.

Vashtan took another sip of tequila, straight from the bottle, then tilted his head back, face to the sky - "Aaaayyyyeeeee!" - he shouted up towards the heavens in his best impression of the classic Mexican *grito*. "Aaah! Aaah! Aaah!" He was laughing hysterically, pounding the table with his hand like a crazed lunatic. "Viva Mexico, Cabrones!!!!!" He screamed again. Mania.

Natalie jumped up from the table, the madness of the moment possessing her, as she grabbed Vashtan's head, pulling his hair before kissing him long and hard, tasting the tequila still on his lips.

They lingered there in the square, kissing and drinking in a hazy stupor, trying their best to help each other forget. Because there was nothing else left to do. It was over.

Then, just when they had reached their lowest

point, threatening to pull each other down into the abyss - a voice came out from directly behind them, an unmistakable American accent floating on the thin, high-altitude Mexican breeze.

"Just one question..."

They spun around, stunned.

"Why do you think the old man wants me dead?"

Then he was gone.

MEXICO CITY, MEXICO

He's alive. Peter Strickland is alive. The thought flashed through his head like a surge of electricity.

Then he threw up. Again.

Vashtan was on his knees in the tiled hotel bathroom, wrapped around the porcelain toilet that at the moment was his best friend. He was staring into the bottom of the bowl and what seemed at the time to be the infinite bowels of the universe. He flushed again and watched dizzily as the regurgitated remains of last night's debauchery swirled off into the vast piped underbelly of the Mexican capital. What other filth must be swimming down there? He pondered the question briefly, before another bout of nausea forced him to expel the last of his stomach contents. This time it was just acid and bile, burning the back of his throat, and eliciting a follow-up response of uncomfortably audible gagging and spitting.

"You OK in there?" Natalie called out from the adjacent room.

Vashtan spit again. "Fucking fantastic."

He got up slowly from the floor and looked in the mirror. His hair was a sweaty tangled mess, pushed to one side and smeared across his forehead like a spiderweb. His shirt was a vomit-stained patchwork of reds and yellows, thanks to an overabundance of salsa and grilled *elote* corn purchased drunkenly from the road-side vendors on Paseo de la Reforma. He winced at his current state of affairs, then ducked his head under the sink faucet, rinsing out his mouth and slicking back his straight brown hair. He splashed some more cold water on his face before peeling off his putrid undershirt, and then walked out the bathroom door.

Natalie was stretched out on top of the hotel duvet, watching a Mexican news broadcast coming from the old rectangular TV at the foot of the bed. She was not sick.

"Did you get it all out?"

"And then some, I think."

"Sure sounded like it."

Vashtan winced again. "Tequila," he said - stating the obvious.

"And maybe some adrenaline." Natalie added.

She was right. It wasn't *just* the tequila (although it certainly played its part). It was also the shock of talking to a dead man just hours after you saw him gunned down and nearly decapitated right before your eyes. It had all happened right there. There was no way that man could have survived.

And that man obviously did not. But that man was also not Peter Strickland.

In hindsight it was all perfectly clear. Strickland knew they were coming, and had hired a decoy. Perhaps it was just a ploy to draw them out, confuse them maybe. Or just a little sleight of hand to sneak off into the vault while their heads were turned. Either way, he couldn't have known it would turn out like that. Could he???

And what did he mean by *the old man wants me dead*?

Vashtan and Natalie had spent the better part of the morning debating the how's and the why's of the situation, trying to get a handle on why Strickland had even come to them at all. Why not just run? Obviously it was only a matter of time before the authorities put a name to the faceless remains of the body on the street in Polanco. It would have to come out eventually. Why let them know beforehand and risk everything?

And then there was the central question. Who *exactly* wanted Strickland dead? Who ordered the hit? Was it all part of some elaborate set-up?

They didn't have any answers.

It had all happened so fast, Strickland had come out of nowhere, just like another one of Vashtan's apparitions. He had only spoken to them briefly, just long enough to give them a few curt instructions, before disappearing into the faceless Garibaldi crowds. He had stunned them. And in their shock and drunken stupor they hadn't had time to react. He had probably planned that too.

In any case, they'd get their answers soon enough. Or at least they hoped they would.

Strickland had left a note at their hotel: he'd meet them in Xochimilico at the Carmelita barge at two PM tomorrow. But there were detailed instructions to be followed first.

Vahstan had been popping excedrin pills all morning, the aching pain in his head slowly abating as the combination of aspirin, acetaminophen and caffeine finally started to take effect. Eventually he felt stable enough to go out, and headed down to the little sports store a few blocks away where he bought himself a Pumas soccer jersey, then had the number 99 stencilled on the back. Natalie had already finished her assignment, picking up a white sunhat, yellow sandals and a bundle of purple hydrangeas.

They'd be fairly easy to spot.

As Vashtan wandered back towards their hotel, the numbered jersey in a plastic drawstring bag slung over his shoulder, he passed another one of the stalls selling *elote*, slathered in mayonnaise and sprinkled liberally with bright red chili. He caught a smell of the grilled corn on the cob as it wafted up from the metal stand, paused for a moment, and then hustled off toward his room as fast as he could.

The nausea was back.

FLORENCE, ITALY

The Professor was anxious as he paced up and down along the pebble-strewn path that bisected the villa garden. Uneven rays of light streamed through the thinning grape leaves of the vine covered pergola, the little fruit that remained now shrivelled into tiny purple raisins, clumped into bunches and suspended awkwardly overhead. The Professor could feel the beginnings of winter in the air, minute stabbings of icy pinpricks brushing the tips of his fingers, on his nose and on his ears. It was too soon, thought the Professor, too soon to be this cold. He was slightly perturbed by the physical sensation, but more deeply affected by the prematurity of the meteorological phenomenon itself. The seasons, though fickle, tended to respect the underlying rhythms of nature. When they did not: chaos. And as the Professor knew all too well, timing was everything.

It was timing that was on the Professor's mind as he strolled through the garden, the weak late-autumn sun fading low in the distance, casting a reddish-orange glow across the evening sky. '*Rosso di sera, bel tempo si spera...*' He remembered the old Italian proverb. '*Red sky at night, sailor's delight*' the rough English equivalent. Maybe so, he thought, but this time it was just as likely to mean blood.

In the past day the Professor had made what was, for him, a stunning miscalculation. It was an error driven by over-exuberance, a shocking mistake more typical of a novice than of an experienced player such as himself. In short, he had moved too quickly.

Instead of waiting for third party confirmation of Strickland's demise, he had trusted the Catalan to be good to his word and had hastily set the wheels in motion. And now to stop it, there would be a price to pay. A price not denominated in euros, dollars, pounds or francs.

No, this price would be one of flesh. And of bone.

But whatever the costs may be, they would have

to be paid. With the whispers reaching him that the body in Mexico City was not Peter Strickland, the Professor knew that the risks had become too great. Making a rash gambit at this stage could prove to be his undoing. Strickland was no fool and had already beaten him once before. He was a savvy operator. A player. And a fellow player was never to be underestimated.

Yes, the mistake would be costly, he thought. But what choice did he have? Everything was predicated on perfect timing.

And now, the timing was all wrong.

The Professor continued his nervous pacing, then suddenly stopped. He placed his acacia-wood cane up against a thick stone post, echo of an Etruscan past, then clasped his hands behind his back and exhaled slowly.

As he calmly surveyed his surroundings, he knew there was nothing to be done. They would have to be sacrificed.

"*Peccato,*" the Professor sighed. "Such a shame."

A pair of jet-black ravens chased one another through a patch of winter squash, the faded yellow blossoms the only sign of life in the otherwise desolate garden.

The Professor breathed in deeply, the frosty air tickling the lining of his nostrils. Then he closed his eyes tight to stymie the suggestion of a sneeze, and concentrated on his re-calculations.

Yes, the board had now been rearranged, he thought. The Catalan would be forced to stay in Mexico just a little while longer and thus could be of no use to him here. But the beauty of the game was that were always other pieces. And luckily for him, there was still another knight on the board. Yes, there was another.

The Professor reached for his cane, the apian signet ring on his finger tapping against the smooth, gently knotted wood. Then he turned down the pebble-lined path and briskly walked inside.

He would have to inform the man in the dark suit.

MADRID, SPAIN

Abdullah pulled back the hood of his dark sweatshirt as he stepped into the narrow, dimly lit staircase that led up to his shared flat. The entrance, on a steep side-street just west of the Lavapies metro station, was located behind a Bangladeshi mini-market that specialised in fresh produce (as well as shadily obtained disposable SIM cards for long distance phone calls). Jogging up the steps to the third floor, Abdullah turned left to number 6 and pressed the buzzer, then knocked four times in two distinct pairings. The door opened slowly inward and Abdullah slipped quickly through the nearly too-tight opening before immediately closing the door behind him.

At the round plastic table in the middle of the room sat three of his roommates. A fourth man stood sentry next to the now closed front door. On the top of the table a portable sterno stove kit was heating a beige-coloured paste in a small metal pot. The other men did not look up when he entered, instead concentrating on the cooking substance that made a slight hissing sound as it delicately bubbled on the surface.

Abdullah walked up and took from his pocket the folded piece of paper that he had received from the light-skinned men in the square and placed it down with a theatrical flourish next to the sterno.

"The Balkan ones have delivered on their promise. Alhamdulillah." There was pride in his voice.

The others in the room did not respond. They were still absorbed with the nearly-boiling sludge.

"Did you not hear me, my brothers? The weapons. It is just as I promised. They are here!"

"Sshhh! Silence!" came the response, as the skinny one carefully stirred the mixture, more tiny bubbles now coming to the surface.

Abdullah was offended but did not say a word, lest he upset the delicate work of his 'brothers' around the table.

After a few minutes, when the substance had reached the proper consistency, the small flame was extinguished and the attention could now be turned to Abdullah, who had retreated impishly to his small sleeping cot, one of five placed haphazardly around the rubbish strewn and smelly single room.

The skinny one spoke again. "So you bring us good news?"

"Yes, it is very good news indeed. Last night I received a call from the old man. We shall have the weapons. Insha'Allah."

"Insha'Allah," replied the skinny one.

"On the table are the license plate numbers," Abdullah explained, the pride now showing in his voice. "We must go to the garage, just as before. The car will be parked there, level two. Under the lining in the boot we will find the tools we require. Just as I promised."

The skinny one opened the folded piece of paper on the table. CR 153 032

"It is indeed as you promised, Abdullah. God smiles on his servant."

Abdullah bowed his head slightly, before beaming towards the floor.

"All is nearly in place." The skinny one continued in a louder voice, standing up at the table now and raising his arms high above his head: "Yes, we are ready, my brothers. Soon we will strike another giant blow against the infidel. After more than five and one quarter centuries since our people were last driven from this land, the time has finally come to restore the rule of our Prophet!"

The predictable response came shouted in unison. "Allahu Akbar! Allahu Akbar!"

But one man did not shout, instead reflecting on the license number while he stood silently guarding the door. CR 153 032. Corps Diplomatique. Diplomatic tags. And not just any diplomatic tags either.

The big man who they called Faris - and who to them was nothing more than a muscle-bound bodyguard - had seen those numbers before. Yes, he had definitely seen them before. Unconsciously flexing the trapezius muscles at the base of his neck and shrugging his shoulders forward, the powerfully built Faris opened his green-flecked eyes wide in sudden recognition of the significance of the numbers, and then smiled inwardly to himself.

"Change of plans, brothers," he thought. "Alhamdullilah."

BRUSSELS, BELGIUM

T he man in the dark suit hung up the phone, then turned to face the tall windows that looked out over the manicured green lawns of the Parc Leopold. He thrust his hips out, a little farther than usual this time, and shoved his hands deep into his pockets as he watched the swans swimming, two-by-two in the deep blue pond just past the trees.

"Ahhh dear Professor," he sighed to himself, shaking his head slowly from side to side. "You are out of practice my friend."

He looked up at the little grey storm clouds moving rapidly across the open azure sky and wondered if he had chosen the right partner.

The reality was that he still did not trust the Professor, not quite yet. They had only just begun and already there was a misstep. And a rather sophomoric one at that. Perhaps the Professor's famed acumen was fading.

But it wasn't so much the Professor's skills that he doubted, but rather his motivations. There was something strange about his sudden reappearance. Something that he could not quite put his finger on. It troubled him.

No, he would not trust the Professor. Not until he was sure.

Surprisingly, the Professor had come to him on his own with this latest development. It must have taken a certain amount of humility to admit his mistake, and he had never known the Professor to be a humble man.

That too, was strange.

But no matter, for now their work would continue, in spite of everything. There was simply too much to be gained, and anyway the loss was acceptable.

The man in the dark suit turned sharply on his heels, the light through the clouds casting long shadows on the sterile marble floor in front of him. He walked over to the corner of his spacious office, where a large globe rested ponderously atop a solid beechwood base. He opened the northern hemisphere to reveal a fairly well-stocked bar, and then poured himself a generous glass of inky-dark 1970 Fonseca Vintage Port.

"Just a little reinforcement," he thought.

After all, there would soon be a crisis in Madrid that would require his attention.

He took a few moments, enjoying the deep complexity of his drink and the way it slid over his tongue like a sweet velvet glove. Then he headed alone down the labyrinthine corridors, accompanied only by the click-clack echoes of his freshly polished shoes.

MADRID, SPAIN

His left bicep bulged out menacingly, stretching the fabric of his plain grey T-shirt as he checked the black rubber Casio G-Shock on his left wrist. "Right on schedule," Faris thought to himself.

The group of Arab men he had been watching were exiting the little market in front of the apartment and heading up the road towards the metro stop. He knew they were giddy now, as they marched in single file behind the skinny one with his goofy loping stride. They were excited to be on the cusp of completing their mission for Allah. As Faris watched them, he grinned with satisfaction because he knew something that they did not. Those poor, ignorant bastards.

There would be no weapons waiting for them, no car with license tags CR 153 032. That had been a coded message for him alone. Instead the Arabs would be surprised to find nothing more than an empty parking garage.

And when they returned home there would be an even bigger surprise waiting for them. A much bigger surprise.

Faris punched in the code for the remote timer, activating the trigger mechanism on the device he had placed in the middle of the small room. It was only a matter of time now. He walked leisurely to the little tapas bar on the corner that specialised in the Galician cuisine that he loved so much and ordered a small dish of *pulpo a la gallega* and a tall bottle of crisp, sweet golden cider. Faris attached the plastic double-spouted nozzle to the top of the bottle and poured himself a small amount from an arm's length distance into a wide shallow glass. After a short wait his octopus arrived, sprinkled with salt and the deep red paprika called *pemento picante*. Drizzled lightly with olive oil, it was a dish to savour. Faris allowed himself another glass of cider, the thin stream of liquid jetting forcefully out from the bottle as he poured from an even greater height this time. Still, he did not spill a drop.

An hour later he was still sitting in the booth by the window, his table clean but for the little puddles of condensation where his glass and bottle once stood. When he heard the unmistakable sound of an explosion in the distance, he promptly paid the '*cuenta*' and then headed out to the street where he caught a taxi to the airport in Barajas.

Sitting in the cab as it headed out of town, Faris instinctively rolled his powerful shoulders forward, squeezing his lattisimus dorsi and then pectorals, slowly flexing the muscles in his upper body, working one group against the other like a rippling jungle cat.

He could see the thin plume of smoke rising up as he looked back on the city fading behind him, a sly grin reappearing on his face.

"All too easy."

BARCELONA, SPAIN

F aris sat up and surveyed his surroundings with contentment. Everything was just as he remembered: the large square shaped room filled with heavy, black-iron discs, the thin corrugated metal roof, and the piles of spit and sawdust that covered the concrete floor. The smell was heavy with pheromones, and the flickering fluorescent lamps gave the room a horrid, jail-cell atmosphere. Ascetic and intimidating, it was a rough and crude place for rough and crude men.

He was happy to be home.

Breathing in the hot and sweaty gym air through his nose, Faris arched his back and then exhaled loudly before laying back down on the torn-vinyl weight bench. He lay there prone and motionless for just a moment, listening to the pinging of the rain overhead, then reached up and placed his middle fingers on the grooves of the iron bar suspended above his head. He paused briefly, gazing skyward in concentration, then let out a loud 'HUP!' as he lifted the massive weight off its moorings, fixing it squarely above his chest. Slowly he lowered the imposing weight toward him, inhaling deeply, until the middle of the bar touched his solar plexus, then he hoisted it up hard and smooth, the sound of his exhaled "shhhhhhhh" echoing around the dank, smelly room. He continued the movements until he felt his elbows wobble at the eighth repetition, the pain burning through his triceps and across his chest. He replaced the bar and shouted in satisfaction, then leaned his head between his knees as he stared at the floor in silent contemplation.

Aside from a moustachioed Iranian curling dumbbells in front of a chipped mirror far away in the corner, Faris was alone with his thoughts. Every break in his lifting was a short meditation, his mind cleared from the simple force of his physical exertions. There were no distractions, just the dancing of the rain and the occasional thud of iron on concrete. It was the perfect place to reflect and recompose.

It had always been that way for Faris, his hulking musculature a testament to that fact. But his size and strength had not always been such. Far from it. Instead, a lifetime of monkish devotion had transformed his once frail frame into the imposing specimen that he was now. Twenty years of self-imposed hard labor.

At the age of 13 he had found an outlet for his seething anger and a place of serenity for his expansive mind.

It was a place far away from the cruel world that had battered his empty childhood. A place to forget all the depredations of the past. It was a place where he was not weak, but instead could move mountains. The gym was his source of satisfaction. And his sanctuary.

But he had not found it on his own.

He had come to Barcelona with his family from the shattered Balkans at the time of their deep troubles. A broken family from a broken land - they were the poor outsiders. And easy prey for the established groups of less-than-salubrious types that haunted the Catalan capital at the time: the North African illegals, the gypsy hustlers, the Pakistani gangsters and wanna-be radicals. Crowded down in the Barrio Chino between the halal meat sellers and the cheap electronics stores, it was an underworld of curry and falafel and crime. Faris never stood a chance.

Then one September day, during the festival of *La Merce'* - while the '*correfoc*' parade wreaked havoc on the city streets with its flaming devils shooting fire and sparks into the wild ecstatic crowds - fate intervened. Young Faris had caught a spark in his eye (not an uncommon thing, truth be told) and, temporarily blinded, he had wandered down a side alley as tears streamed down his face. There in a little cobbled road, he was set upon by the Moroccans. They were skinny, and feral, and always worked in packs. They recognised Faris' weakness and attacked him all at once, beating him for sport as the fire-spectacle raged just steps away. The blood poured from his nose, from his elbows, and from his knees as he lay on the paving stones helpless, the blows raining down from all angles.

Then they suddenly stopped. First one, then another of his attackers dropped unconscious - until there were none left standing. Then - like a mirage - a bearded man with close-cropped hair lifted him up gently and took him away.

That was how Faris met Arnau Leport. The man who taught him how to develop his body and mind. How to defend himself. And ultimately, how to kill.

Now he was a full-grown man, and Faris owed his life to the Catalan. He existed in his current incarnation only because of him. Yes, he owed him everything.

And so it was with a deep uncertainty and no small amount of shame that Faris contemplated his latest proposition. It had come to him from an unlikely source this time - and, of course, it was to be another hit. But this one infinitely more delicate than any that had come before. And it would be here. In Barcelona.

Faris tried to empty his thoughts once again as he reclined onto the sweaty vinyl bench. Then he reached up for the bar, lifted the weight, and escaped to that place of no complications, where there was only up and down, and the sound of his "shhhhhhhhhhh" echoing across the hard, rough room.

XOCHIMILCO, MEXICO CITY

Pete Strickland woke up to the smell of tomatoes, garlic, onions and chiles and the sound of fresh tortillas frying in oil. Four eggs sat on the countertop, next to a saucer of cream and a tall pile of snow-white *queso fresco*. A ripe, almost purple, avocado was waiting to be sliced, while a bunch of fresh jagged coriander and a bright green lime shared space in a painted ceramic bowl. The hum of a female voice wafted from the kitchen, as two delicate hands cracked open the eggs to be fried in hot lardo. Anna Maria was making *chilaquiles*.

For Pete Strickland it was a kind of paradise. This worn down little shack with its spartan white stucco walls. The little *alebrije* figurines from down in Oaxaca the only decorations, placed strategically into the nooks and crannies of the thick curving walls. But more than anything else, it was the smell. The smell of a Mexico that reminded him of languid vacations, cold beers on a Pacific beach, course sand in his toes, and salt air in his nostrils. The smell of fresh fish and lime and sticky fingers and tequila. There was no other smell like that in the entire world. Pete breathed it in deeply, because he knew it would not last.

Anna Maria called out to him from the other room.

"Yes, thank you," he shouted back. "A michelada would be fine." One last Mexican beer cocktail before the game got serious once again. On second thought, better make that two. Pete breathed in deeply one more time. Ahhhh.

Then he took a piece of yesterday's newspaper and wrote the message.

Two hours later, Mark Vashtan and Natalie Chalmers exited the Xochimilco light rail and made their way down to the canals that meandered around the man-made islands called *chinampas*. Colourfully decorated gondola-like barges, *trajineras,* ferried around the wide-eyed tourists and the celebrating locals, while floating vendors hawked food and impromptu entertainment. It was a festive and beautiful place.

Vashtan and Natalie walked along the canals' edge looking for the Carmelita barge, the one Strickland told them to find. They were dressed just as he'd instructed, walking hand in hand carrying the large bouquet of flowers. Vashtan felt silly - and just more than a little bit exposed. Natalie on the other hand was surprisingly tranquil. So tranquil in fact that it made Vashtan uneasy.

Did she not understand the risk they were taking? Or maybe she was just that smooth.

Either way, he didn't like it.

They walked for about ten minutes, then Vashtan spotted it. The Carmelita. He gave Natalie a gentle nudge and she smiled at him knowingly from the corner of her mouth. As they approached, his heart began to race and he could feel the moisture building up in his palms, Natalie's hand hot inside his. Just a few more steps.

Then suddenly they were there, the opening to the barge just in front of them. But there was no sign of Strickland. Just a droopy eyed farmer with a bundle of lettuce sitting idly by the side of the big, colourful boat.

"Fuck, it's a set-up," Vashtan thought out loud as he looked around frantically, searching for the bullet that was certain to come. It had to be a trap.

Strickland had played them - and now they were perfect targets.

He flinched, and Natalie gripped his hand tighter. "Just wait..." she whispered.

But nothing happened.

They stood there as the seemingly slow-motion pantomime of normal life played out around them. A man walking his dog. Two children playing in the grass. Young lovers sharing an ice cream.

Then the farmer with the droopy eyes got up slowly and walked towards them, his stride slow and easy. He said nothing as he handed them a folded up piece of newspaper, then he gathered up his lettuce and walked away.

Natalie unfolded the piece of newspaper. On it was circled an article dated from the day before: "Accidental explosion kills suspected terrorists in the heart of Madrid"

Then below, one word written in bloc capitals. BARCELONA.

BARCELONA, SPAIN

A languid Mediterranean breeze wafted through the open doors of El Xampanyet, the fresh air mixing pleasantly with the faintly sour smell of overcrowded human bodies, Spanish ham, and spilled champagne. Pete Strickland stood crowded into a back corner of the bar, his bottle of sparkling *cava rosada* perched precariously on a tiled ledge, fistful of *jamon bocadillo* in one hand, a glass of pink bubbly (the speciality of the house) sloshing out of the side of his shallow glass in the other. Pete took a bite of his sandwich and a quick swish of cava, then glanced around again at the mass of humanity packed into the little tapas joint in the Born quarter of the Catalan metropolis.

He was annoyed.

A tiny bead of sweat dripped down the nape of his neck, the moisture cool on his skin as it evaporated through his button-down beige shirt, adding his own little contribution to the sticky humidity that was slowly filling the room.

It was 2 in the afternoon during the peak rush of a late Spanish lunch, and his man was late.

Pete would give him another quarter-hour, nothing more. This was a risky move to begin with and there was no guarantee he would even show up. The proposition was certainly a bold one and not to be taken lightly. But it was the only play he had left.

It was time to lay his cards on the table.

The business in Madrid had forced his hand. He knew that it had been a warning shot - the next time, well, the next time innocent people would die. And Pete couldn't have that on his conscience. Not when he could do something about it. But after everything that had happened, now he'd have to play against the odds. From here on out there could be no counting on luck. This would be a game of skill. And there was no room for error.

He'd left a trail of bread crumbs for Vashtan and

Chalmers back in Mexico. Actually not so much bread crumbs - more like a giant roadmap. They would follow him here, that much was certain. But he wondered how much they actually knew and if they were aware they were just pawns on the big board. No, they certainly didn't know the whole story...

Leport, the Catalan, would track them again just as he always did. Pete knew the tradecraft. He had practically invented it back when they'd all gotten rich off the largesse floating around North Africa back during the latest round of almost-secret Western government-financed unpleasant-ness. That had been low-hanging fruit, and a good gig...until certain people got greedy. And a bit too comfortable with spilling blood.

Pete was always amazed by the facility that wealthy people had with accepting the misfor-tune of others in the service of their own financial gain. But he had never been an idealist, and knew that was just the way of things.

The way they had always been.

Fortunes had always been built on the sweat of the oppressed. And on their blood. But as far as he was concerned, you were either the hammer or the nail. Which one was mostly up to you.

But Pete could only take it so far. Callousness and a little bit of injustice were one thing - - wholesale murder was another. He wasn't that kind of villain.

That was why he had gotten out all those years ago. And he had stayed out until that day on the beach in Belize when they had come back for him.

He knew there was only one reason they'd want him dead. Only one reason they'd take the risk of pulling him out of his self- imposed hibernation and back into the game.

They were back in business.

And Pete knew the players. They were the shadow operators who had cut their teeth in Africa back before his time, trading in arms, black gold and favours, until the Elf scandal had hit the presses in Europe and forced them into a temporary re-treat. But the vultures had never left the African shadows, preying on the corpse of that dark con-tinent while the rest of the world silently forgot.

Pete was a player in their world for a number of years, complicit in their schemes, another cog in the dirty wheel of money, power, and intrigue.

But that was another time.

Now, it seemed, they were taking their business back home. And upping the stakes.

The timing was right, the collective mood of the general population likely conducive now to their crude manipulations. They were smart, that arrogant cabal, and could probably sense that the pendulum was primed to shift. Just a few explosive shoves in the right direction...

Pete grimaced.

He couldn't live with just letting them get away with it. Not this time. There wasn't enough money in all the banks in Switzerland to keep him quiet. He had already learned the hard way that his conscience was not for sale. And this wild gambit was his chance to finally sleep soundly.

But where was his man??? If he didn't walk through that door in the next 15 minutes, it would be over before it even started.

Pete downed the rest of his cava rosada, and poured himself another as the din of noise in the bar rose to a crescendo, a boisterous group of sandalled Germans now packing the windowed entrance.

Then he saw him pushing his way through the tight crowd. A hulking mass, a veritable man among boys, those familiar ripped biceps stretching the sleeves of his tight black shirt.

Pete gave him a subtle nod from the back of the room, and the man approached. Pete poured a glass.

"Hello Faris" he said, the accent hard and percussive on the F. "I'm glad you came. Have you made a decision?"

"My answer is yes."

"Excellent. That's good news. Let's you and me talk some business."

"*Paciencia*, my friend. First we shall drink."

"Ah, a man after my own heart." Pete responded, pouring a glass for Faris. "Salut then..."

Faris tilted his head slightly downward, looking Pete directly in the eyes, without even a hint of emotion in his own. Then he raised his glass.

"*Txin txin.*"

TUSCANY, ITALY

The sleek 1976 Alfa Romeo Spider jolted down the gravel packed '*strada bianca*' just outside Montalcino, heading southwest through the rose flecked vineyards of the Val d'Orcia, past hidden estates lined with cypress trees, and toward the peninsula called Argentario, its craggy nooks jutting proudly out into the pristine waters of the Mediterranean.

This was certainly not the fastest route from Florence to Porto Santo Stefano - infinitely slower than the autostrada or even the old two-lane state roads - but the Professor had a deep fondness for the hidden parts of his native land. He knew these twisting and gnarled paths from his youth, the little bits of rubble poking eerily from unkempt farmland, signposts of Etruscan treasures lurking just beneath the surface. He remembered his uncle telling him to "always follow the white roads," where the wonders of the countryside opened themselves up to chance discoveries.

You could never get that on a highway, the Professor thought. Those paved scars only served to cut through his ancient land, cleaving a path irrespective of the history or culture surrounding it. Such a shame.

No, the Professor would always take the 'white roads' even as his little 1976 Spider took a beating on the unfinished tracks. His back ached and his forearms were sore from the constant jostling and the repeated, yet still unpredictably angry dips in the road.

But there would be rewards too - a glass of *Rosso di Montalcino* from an old friend's vines, or a taste of homemade wild boar sausage. They were small pleasures, no doubt, but they held an almost mystic sway over the professor. He knew these vestiges of the past were slipping away, being slowly killed by the trappings of modernity. So he relished every moment out here in the countryside. Communing with the past was his path to spirituality. And on these rare occasions when circumstance brought him out here to his church the emotions would be profound, yet touched with sadness. Because he could see God disappearing.

As the hills of the valley eased out into the coastal plain of the Maremma, the Professor turned his mind back to the present and toward the future. In Porto Santo Stefano, there would be a boat captain with the name Gregor. It was an oddly non-Italian name that betrayed the political sens- ibilities of his parents. But Gregor himself was not a communist. No, Gregor was only a soldier, con- ditioned to follow orders without question. He would take the Professor to Barcelona where a most unusual meeting awaited him.

The Professor had already played the moves out in his head. It was another gambit forced upon him by Strickland, who continued to prove him- self a most adept player. But it was also a chance to make a decisive move. All the pieces would be there, ripe for the taking. Still, he would have to be cautious. Strickland's objective was as yet not entirely clear, and he couldn't assume to know his motivations. But, as always, he would trust human nature. In that he was always confident.

The sun was slowly setting over the Tuscan archi- pelago in the distance as the Alfa Romeo turned onto the coastal highway outside Orbetello, la- goons flanking both sides of the road. Seagulls danced against the orange horizon and the smell of the sea crept in through the partly open windows. The Professor breathed in the first of many saline-infused breaths to come - and immediately thought of dinner, and the wonderful little spot near the port that served the best *spaghetti alle vongole* in town. There would be wine too, a lightly colored *Ansonica* from the island of Giglio, and a few hours of animated conversation with the old sailors that filled the establishment. Then it would be time to meet Gregor, set sail for the Spanish coast, and resume the game.

BARCELONA, SPAIN

U nseasonably warm, he thought. Spain, or rather Catalunya, was always temperate here at the coast. But at the port, with the wind blowing in from the sea, it could be cold in winter. The journey from the Argentario had been rough, a mild storm churning the water into cloudy tempests, icy darts of rain drilling the boat deck with intermittent violent bursts, dark clouds everywhere on the horizon. It had been a normal winter passage.

But sitting now at the Port Olimpic at a table in the sun, the Professor could tell that the weather had shifted. He leaned his cane against the white table next to the bobbing sailboats and rapped his signet ring on the plastic surface in satisfaction.

He enjoyed being here. Enjoyed the smell of the harbour. Of ocean, brine and gasoline. But most importantly, he enjoyed being back. Now it was only a matter of time.

A waiter came by and took his order: *pa amb tomaquet* (fresh tomato and garlic on bread) and a black coffee. The professor packed his pipe and lit it with a match, sending bagel-shaped clouds of smoke out over the water's edge as he puffed away in contentment.

The waiter returned with a coffee, and laid it down roughly before scurrying away. As the professor was about to take a sip, the chair across from him scraped backward and Pete Strickland sat down.

"Coffee and tobacco, eh? Those are a couple of bad habits you got there old man."

The professor was nonplussed, and took a deep pull on his pipe.

"This is true Mr. Strickland, but they are not the worst. And I imagine you must have a few of your own, is this not so?"

"Yeah, I guess so - but before you think about freeing me of my worldly vices as we like to say, you should know there's a gun on you too. You didn't think I'd come without covering my back, did you?

"No, I did not."

"Good. Let's talk business then."

"And what business might that be, Mr. Strickland?"

"I want out."

"Of course you do, of course you do. But I fail to see how this is possible. As far as I can tell we are at an impasse."

Pete nodded. "I kill you, you kill me. Yeah, I'd say that's an impasse all right. But there's another option."

Pete paused, looking out past the boats in the marina, and to the open sea in the distance.

"And what might that option be, Mr. Strickland?"

"How about we both just walk away from here. No harm, no foul. You go about your business and I won't stop you this time. All I want is to disappear. You have my word as a fellow professional."

"Well that is an interesting proposal, Mr. Strickland. An interesting proposal indeed. But may I first inquire - this gunman you have '*on me*' so to speak, would it happen to be our friend Faris?"

Pete did not respond.

"Oh I am afraid this is all rather embarrassing for you Mr. Strickland." The professor took a few more self-satisfied puffs on his pipe then leaned over the table towards Pete. "Did you not know?"

"Not know what exactly?"

"Faris was made by the Catalan. He is his. And, as you know, the Catalan is *MINE*."

Pete's eyes flinched at the statement, but the Professor did not notice and continued: "How did you think you could turn Faris against us with something so crude as gold? He is a mercenary, true. But just as with you, or myself, or even the Catalan - he is also human. It is as simple as human nature, Mr. Strickland. The Catalan has been mine since I made him, just as Faris is his. Human nature, my friend. Always trust in human nature."

Pete was impassive. "So then you're going to kill me?"

"I am afraid so. You no longer have the package, Mr. Strickland, and thus you are disposable…though it does me no pleasure. You have been an excellent player, and I have so much enjoyed your presence over the years. But I must be going now. As you have already deduced, the Catalan has a rifle on you. I will give you a minute to compose yourself, and to choose the scene with which you depart. This is not such a bad place to say goodbye. There is coffee and tobacco, and the sea sparkling in the distance. A man cannot ask for much more. And, as you just said, all you want is to disappear. Call it a professional courtesy...*arrivederci*, Mr. Strickland"

The Professor grabbed his cane, but did not get up. Something was not as it should be.

Pete smiled. "You're great at the strategy old man, but you're rusty on the playing field. I had hoped for this, but honestly I had been expecting more."

The Professor slumped slightly in his flimsy plastic chair, the colour draining out of his face. "You knew Faris would betray you?"

"I knew you would try to fuck me over. Just like you said - human nature."

"And why should I not just kill you now then?"

Pete stared at him, "You know why."

The Professor's mind suddenly flashed back to the board - and he instantly recognised his mistake.

"The pawns..."

The words were not even out of his mouth, yet he already knew.

He had been beaten.

A few hundred metres north of the port, past the shuttered *chirinquito* beach bars and just off the water's edge, Natalie Chalmers flipped the switch on the communication equipment resting on the control panel of the little vessel, then nodded back at Mark Vashtan.

"Did you get that?"

"I got it."

With that, Vashtan turned the rudder, swinging the zodiac boat in a big arc back out to sea. They had everything they needed.

Strickland had been right.

The game had changed.

BRUSSELS, BELGIUM

The man in the dark suit dropped his head slightly as he swivelled his office chair back out towards the view over the park in the distance. He listened intently, a scowl slowly spreading across his face, as the bad news continued over the other end of the line.

After a few moments his response came, curt with more than a hint of agitation.

"Bring the old man to me."

He stood up and walked slowly over to the old cartographer's globe in the corner. Then continued his instructions.

"And send the Catalan to Amsterdam. Sanitation protocol."

He opened the northern hemisphere and perused the bottles lining the interior of the hidden bar.

This calls for something a little stronger.

Settling on a single-estate *Le Peu* cognac, amber coloured and richly aromatic, the man in the dark suit poured himself a healthy glass and returned to his oversized leather chair.

Swirling the liquid in his bulbous glass and enjoying the vapours, he looked out admiringly over the Parc Leopold. To him it was perfection. Orderly and manicured, and a complete contrast with the mess created by the Professor's ineptitude.

"Unacceptable," he thought to himself.

The news from the other end of the line had been incomplete. But it was enough to know that the trigger had not been pulled. Whatever the reason may be, it was still a failure.

The man in the dark suit reflected on how patient he had been. Indeed, he had given the Professor more chances than he deserved. The window for action was closing, and costing him money with each passing day.

He would wait no more.

If the Professor could not remove the obstacle in his path, then unfortunately it was the Professor who had now become the obstacle.

But the man in the dark suit had no patience for obstacles.

And so in a few days' time there would be no more.

He took another sip of the cognac, savouring the delicate burn on the back of his tongue and throat, and opened the humidor sitting on his cherry-wood desk. He pulled out a dark brown Arturo Fuente Opus X cigar, ran it quickly under his short nose, and then slipped it inside his vest pocket.

He got up and proceeded out to his next round of budget meetings, the long white marble corridor now filled with the click-clack echo of his freshly polished shoes.

FIESOLE, ITALY

nderneath a dome-shaped pergola at the end of a long pebbled path, the Professor, Faris, and the Catalan huddled over a squat travertine table near a tall stone wall. Pine trees and cypresses mixed along the steep road below, and in the distance the lights of Florence twinkled invitingly in the autumnal dusk.

The Catalan spoke first.

"Why?"

The Professor knew of course that this would be the query, and his answer was pre-prepared, albeit purposefully opaque.

"A piece on the board is not to be removed lightly. Nor only because it can be taken. It must always serve some greater purpose, later in the game."

Faris snorted and looked away. He never understood the Professor's moves anyway, let alone his philosophising, and to him it was enough to follow orders and watch the dominoes fall. He couldn't care less about Pete Strickland.

The Catalan, on the other hand, had been following Strickland for weeks now, and was clearly more invested in the outcome. He was personally offended by the developments in Barcelona and would not be satisfied with another empty proverb from his guru. He needed to know more. His protege Faris might be just another piece in the game - but the Catalan? No, the Catalan wanted to be a player.

"What purpose?"

The Professor shifted his acacia-wood cane in Leport's direction, an ice-cold stare directed straight into the Catalan's eyes.

"Do you trust me?"

"Always."

"Then you will know...when the time is right."

The Catalan nodded solemnly and swallowed his pride. It was not what he wanted to hear, but he would accept it. The Professor had earned that much. Still, he would speak his mind.

"The man in the dark suit should be informed."

At the mention of the man in the dark suit, Faris returned to the conversation. "He knows."

The Professor wrinkled his eyes and immediately took off his spectacles, placing them gently on the round stone table before turning his attention to Faris.

"And may I ask how he knows?"

"I informed him."

"Is that so?"

"Yes."

"And if I may be so bold, dear Faris, why *exactly* did you inform him?"

Faris' response was simple and to the point. "Because I am paid to."

The Professor was calm and measured as he replied. There was no hint of shock, nor disappointment - only a very bland "*certo*, of course."

The Catalan, less skilled at concealing his emotions than the Professor, was unnerved at this apparent lack of respect. He glared decisively at Faris, and did not ask, but rather demanded, in no uncertain terms, to know the extent of the conversation with the man in the dark suit.

Faris, accustomed as always to following orders, was not taken aback by Leport's verbal aggression and responded immediately.

"You are being sent to Amsterdam. The radicals are to be eliminated. Full sanitation."

The Catalan continued his demands. "Sanitation?" His surprise was evident. "So the operation is to be aborted?"

Faris instinctively flexed the muscles at the base of his neck, his powerful shoulders rolling slightly forward.

"This I do not know. I am to accompany the Professor to Brussels for further instructions."

"Further instructions?" The Catalan was confused.

But the Professor understood almost instantly.

"*Certo* - - of course..."

With this the old man retrieved his spectacles from the stone table, pulled up the collar of his grey Aquascutum trench-coat, and walked slowly back down the pebbled path...the scenarios slowly beginning to take shape in his mind.

ROME, ITALY

Vashtan awoke with a start, the violent end to his recurring nightmare jolting him out of his intermittent slumber. As usual, he had slept poorly - yet another lingering effect from the years of mental trauma.

Turning sideways in bed, he wiped the angst from his mind, then ran a hand down the long arch of Natalie's back, a gentle caress that was reciprocated with the sideways smile that always worked.

"Coffee?"

"Mmmm…yes please," she purred back, almost seductively but not quite.

Vashtan walked the few paces over to the stainless steel galley kitchen, and the lone appliance on the long metal counter. A wood-panelled La Marzocco espresso machine, sleek yet powerful, the race-car of morning beverage makers, it waited solemnly for his expert manipulations. A hiss here, a hiss there - and it was done - two small coffees each with a rich, perfectly formed *schiuma*.

"Perfetto..."

Vashtan drank his in a single quaff at the counter, Italian-style, and carried the second porcelain espresso cup back to Natalie, who was sitting up in bed, watching the British news on a flat-panel TV against the far wall.

"So..." he began with the central question they both had to answer for themselves, "do you believe him?"

Natalie took a tiny sip of coffee, then threw a single leg over the side of the bed.

"I wouldn't have, if I hadn't heard the Professor say the words himself...*the catalan is mine*..."

"I guess that's why Strickland risked everything in Barcelona - he had to make the old man say it."

"And make sure we heard."

"Still..." Vashtan was of course dubious. "I'm not so sure. You know he hasn't got the best track record for integrity."

"Who, Strickland? That's true," Natalie nodded, "but then in our line of work who really does?"

Vashtan knew she was right. This game they were playing was a maze, a house of mirrors. There was no such thing as integrity, or honesty, or the truth.

He should have known that, and instead he had been burned by the Professor, who had played him for a pawn. He felt like a fool for playing checkers when he should have been playing chess.

He was angry, furious even. But there was no room for sentiment, and no time for vacillation. If Pete Strickland were to be believed, the wheels were already in motion.

Natalie had spent the previous night digesting Strickland's story, the hidden meaning behind seemingly random events now coming into crystalline focus. At least for her, it all made sense. The Catalan connection to the unfolding events previously obscure, now abundantly clear.

She was ready to trust Strickland and to make the next move...whatever that might be.

Vashtan on the other hand had yet to be convinced...to him there was still something missing. Something that he could not quite put his finger on.

Still, was his uncertainty enough to risk the consequences that Pete Strickland was so sure were on the horizon?

There were no easy answers, he thought to himself, and it was still too early for whiskey.

"Damn."

At a luxury hotel on the Via Veneto, near the American embassy and tucked between the expanse of the Villa Borghese to the north and the Bernini-adorned Piazza Barberini to the south, Pete Strickland had taken a suite under the name Brad Jackson.

Two half-empty glasses of Bollinger champagne, one stained with a cherry-red lipstick, sat abandoned on a little table over an intricate Persian carpet under an enormous crystal chandelier.

Pete stood robed in the open window, watching the pedestrians scurry up and down the former heart of Italy's *La Dolce Vita,* now just a dour shadow of its former Hollywood splendour. They all looked alike down there, shapes passing on the sidewalk, furry winter coats and tall boots for the women, suits and overcoats for the men. The mindless automatons of global commerce...

The curtains ruffled around him as a crisp wind pushed down from the hills above the Eternal City, blowing the water from the top of the Fontana del Tritone into a sideways spray out over the traffic-ringed square below.

Pete breathed in the petrol-tinged city air, and thought back to his twenty-dollar-a-night hotel in San Pedro, crumbling and perfect, and that view out over the Caribbean Sea and the reef in the distance. That was the life he wanted. The life he wanted to return to.

And anyway, luxury hotels always made him feel like he was at work.

Walking back into the suite and opening the front door, he allowed his guest to depart silently, before retrieving the *il Messagero* newspaper tucked inside a plastic sleeve hanging from the gold-plated door handle.

He returned inside to the plush couch near the bed, put his feet up on the glass-topped coffee table, and opened the paper to a story on the stalled EU budget negotiations rankling the eurocrats in the halls of Brussels.

As he turned a crisp page, there was a ring from the hotel phone on the bedside table.

"Mr. Jackson, *c'è un messaggio qui per te.*"

A message.

Pete hung up the phone and hurried into the large wardrobe to prepare for the day ahead. It was time to get back to work.

Down in the lobby, a man with close-cropped dark hair brushed past the uniformed doorman and through the rotating portal into the late morning sunshine. Putting on his gold-rimmed aviator sunglasses and zipping up his black leather jacket, he walked down the Via Veneto before disappearing into the *Linea A* metro, two stops from Termini Station and the express train for Fiumicino Airport.

BRUSSELS, BELGIUM

On a dark alley tucked off the Rue des Bouchers, a muscle-bound man dressed in black took a second sip of beer and nodded as his table companion got up to leave.

It was the second time in two weeks that someone had asked Faris to kill the Professor. The first time had merely been a proposal.

This one was an order.

There would be no protection for the old man now. He had played his last hand in Barcelona, and now the real powers demanded their retribution. There had been too many mistakes, too much disorder. And now *they* had lost their confidence. It was too much even for the old man to overcome.

And so he would have to pay.

He knew the price - - they all did. In this there was never any doubt.

It was the reason he would follow his orders. The reason the Catalan, although disappointed, would ultimately understand. There were rules to the game - and the rules were always to be followed.

Faris thought back disdainfully on all the Professor's "moves" and on all his convoluted strategies. What a waste. It was so much more simple than that, he thought.

Follow orders. Do your job.

When there is an obstacle, move it. With brute force if need be. The simpler the movement, the stronger you become.

Up.

Down.

Just like in the gym.

The Catalan would certainly be displeased, of course. He had always held the Professor in high regard. Too high, in Faris' opinion. It was that esteem that had ultimately held them back. Now there would be a whole new world of opportunities awaiting them. But the old man would have to go. And the Catalan would adjust.

To Faris it was just that simple, and in that simplicity he found serenity.

An order had been given. And so an order would be followed.

Faris calmly finished the last of his Belgian ale, then watched as the man who had given him his order disappeared down the darkened alley, leaving behind only a shadow and the click-clack echo of freshly polished shoes.

AMSTERDAM, THE NETHERLANDS

A rnau Leport crossed the Herengracht canal in the Jordaan district and headed for his favourite spot in the Dutch metropolis. Here, on the corner of Herenstraat, was a shop that specialised in bespoke canvas bags (among a panoply of other deluxe travel items). The urbane owners always served complimentary espresso coffees to their customers, and curated a counter of high-end fragrances, of which a delicate blend known as *Mémoires De Mustique* was Leport's favourite. The Catalan always stopped here to purchase at least one item on each of his travels to the Netherlands, and although he had business to attend to, he would come here first and complete his customary ritual.

Perusing the offerings of waxed canvas bags and felt-lined portfolios, he ultimately settled on a copper-plated travel pencil - a discrete purchase that he would gladly add to his abundant collection.

He spent a few moments chatting amiably with the staff, enjoying his espresso and doing his best to act the part of the valuable repeat customer.

But in the back of his mind there was always the job looming on the horizon, and as he finished his coffee his hand absentmindedly reached back to touch the black-matte Walther P22 resting securely under his leather jacket.

Just a regular customer, going about his business.

Only an hour earlier he had spoken with the Professor, and the message he had relayed was still fresh in his mind.

There is one who would betray us.

The words had hit him like a punch in the face. Amongst all the sins in the canon of evil, betrayal - betrayal! - that for the Catalan, was the basest and most hideous of them all.

It had taken him only a few moments to understand the meaning of the words the Professor had spoken to him. And that realisation, and the immense depth of that betrayal, was a sickening one. His protege... the one he had rescued, developed, nurtured and instructed...his protege who he had given everything to...

Betrayal.

His hand reached back again to caress the pistol under his jacket, its hard metal edges soothing the raging anger in his soul.

Betrayal.

He gritted his teeth, and pushed the fury to the back of his mind. It would not serve him now.

Because there was still the matter of the job. It was to be sanitation. Or at least that was what he was meant to believe. A simple clean-up, a disposal of loose ends. Only now though, after the message from the Professor, did he understand that he himself was to be one of those loose ends.

Thankfully for him the old man, as always, saw all the angles. There was a reason they were both still alive. One reason only.

It was the brain behind those spectacles, sharpened by years of battle. That brain that saw moves and counter-moves. Not instinctual, but intuitive. There was a difference. A very important difference. Not predator, but player.

And now the move to be played was a delicate one. Delicate and brutal. Everything counted on his guile, and his skills at conjuring destruction. And death.

He had been waiting his whole life for moments like these.

Now it was time to complete his destiny.

And then disappear forever.

Arnau Leport walked back out into the warren of canals in the heart of the city, making his way slowly to Dam Square. From there he caught the number 13 tram, heading west as instructed, to a neighbourhood with a large mosque, and an apartment filled with a small group of Islamic radicals, who had instructions of their own.

He would deal with them in due time, then turn his attention back to his true preoccupation.

Back to the one who had betrayed them.

Back to Faris.

ROME/BRUSSELS

It had been three days since Pete Strickland had passed them the information. Just enough time to organise logistics and get a team in place. Now was the moment of truth.

Vashtan and Natalie made their way through the snarled traffic on the thruway out to the airport in Fiumicino, arriving just in time for the 8:35am Alitalia flight to Brussels. Two hours of flight time, and about 4 Jack Daniels later, they touched down in Belgium and caught a taxi into the city centre, where they'd booked a room in the elegant Amigo Hotel, just off the Grand Place.

Mark Vashtan headed directly for the bar, while Natalie checked them in, under assumed names, and gave a generous tip to the bellhop who ferried their luggage up to a deluxe room on the third floor.

Natalie made her way over to the polished bar and joined Mark who'd already taken the liberty of ordering two drinks and a small platter of olives.

It was 11:30 am.

"Are you ready for this?" She asked him, in spite of the uselessness of the question.

"I better be. It's what I've been doing for the past five years and anyway, the team is ready to go. They're a good group, and they know what to do..."

"So it's just a waiting game at this point?"

"More or less. If Pete Strickland comes through, it should all be over by this afternoon"

"If?" She smiled at him coyly. "You're still not convinced."

"I will be when it's over."

"Will you be satisfied?"

"Satisfied?"

"Yes...with the outcome..."

He took a big, long, deep pull on his drink, adjusted the cocktail napkin on the bar, then looked at Natalie.

"If Pete's right, and that's a big if at this point, I'd be hard pressed to ask for a better outcome." He took another sip of the whiskey. "We'll have averted a major terrorist attack in a European metropolis, the Catalan will be dead, the Professor a marked man with an expiry date, and you and I will have brought in a major player in an international criminal cartel...so satisfied? Yeah, I guess I'd be satisfied."

"And Pete Strickland?"

"Yeah, well...Pete Strickland..."

She put a hand gently on his shoulder.

"He's earned it."

"Yeah, you're probably right...he's played this thing pretty well. At the very least, he's earned the right to walk away on his own terms."

"I think that's all he ever wanted."

"Maybe so, maybe so..." Vashtan's mind was churning. "Still, if *they* are who he says they are, I don't see how they could let him get away. He'd have a target on his back no matter where he went."

"I agree. But who knows what he has in mind? Like you said, he's played this pretty well. So it would make sense that he'd have an exit strategy mapped out. I know I would. Maybe he has some kind of insurance policy, some dirt that they'll want to keep hidden."

"You mean as long as he stays away..."

"Exactly."

They both turned back to face the bar, leaning in close while finishing off their drinks and watching the clock. It was a waiting game now.

❖ ❖ ❖

A short distance away, under a gilded glass arcade…

The news report echoed from the old square television perched atop a plastic stand at the end of a ring of carefully placed cafe tables:

…a number of men were killed when a large explosion rocked the west part of Amsterdam early this morning, after a wide-ranging gun battle in what appeared to be a settling of scores among rival criminal groups. Reports of casualties are sketchy at the moment, but among the dead is reported to be the international terrorist and assassin known as The Catalan…

Pete Strickland looked at the old man, leaning on that worn acacia wood cane, more stooped now than he remembered, and almost felt sorry for him.

Almost.

"So," Pete began. "A deal's a deal."

"Yes, indeed. Yes, indeed." The Professor adjusted

the apian signet ring on his fourth proximal digit, then touched the scar on his face, remembering from whence it came… "My compliments to you, Mr. Strickland. *Chapeau*, as we say. A man must know when he is beaten, and beaten me you have. In other circumstances, if I were bested by another man perhaps…well perhaps I would be more displeased. But in you I have found a worthy adversary. A most worthy adversary. I hope you appreciate the compliment I have given you Mr. Strickland, because I rarely give them, and only in the most extraordinary of circumstances."

"Compliments are all well and dandy," Pete smiled, "But what I'd really appreciate is what we agreed upon in Barcelona. Time to cough it up old man."

"Ah, yes of course…your insurance…"

The Professor reached inside his overcoat and handed Pete Strickland the tightly taped package.

Pete smiled again, this time for real. "And the second part? When and where is this meeting supposed to happen?"

"Place Jourdan. 17:30 precisely."

"Well, it looks like you actually came through old man. Now it's my turn. I'll give them the signal. They'll take care of your problem for you. I don't know how long you'll last after that, but at least it'll give you a head start…"

"Don't worry about me, Mr. Strickland. Perhaps I have an insurance policy of my own."

"Well good for you then."

"One last thing, Mr. Strickland…"

"Call me Pete."

"One last thing Mr. Strickland, Pete. Do the others know, how shall we say, the *exact contents* of the package?"

"Of course not."

"Well then, Mr. Strickland, please take this advice from an old professional: the light and the darkness will continue to do battle, but in the shadows…in the shadows there is always safety." He took off his spectacles and stared directly at his fellow player. "I would not come back if I were you."

"Same goes for you old man."

"To the shadows then."

"*Adios*, Professor."

"*Arrivederci*, Mr. Strickland."

With that Pete turned and headed off toward a black sedan waiting a few hundreds yards away, got in, and made the call.

The Professor walked over to the café tables lining

the indoor sidewalk and took a seat. He ordered a coffee in perfect French, and let the scenarios of his exit play out in his mind.

Faris spotted his prey at the table across the pedestrian boulevard, coffee in hand, sipping in apparent tranquility. It was almost his moment. Faris knew he had only to follow the Professor, making sure that he arrived in time at the agreed-upon meeting with the man in the dark suit. When it was concluded, he'd follow his orders.

He had already identified where he would do it as well, hidden in a shallow walkway behind a shuttered Italian restaurant close to the Hôtel Sofitel. It would be easy work, and then it would be over.

As he was watching the Professor, Faris heard the steps coming from behind him. He turned and immediately recognised the danger. But it was too late. He barely had time to get the words out, "No, wait," before throwing a lumbering punch…but it was too slow.

The man smoothly ducked under Faris' outstretched arm, his head swivelling underneath the armpit as he expertly rotated behind him, chest up tight against Faris' back. It was an elegant move, done effortlessly.

Faris immediately felt the arm reach around his neck, and grabbed it with both hands, pulling down with all his mighty strength. But it was useless.

The man kicked out one of Faris' legs from behind, dragging him backward to the ground as he tightened his grip, forearms squeezing into Faris' carotid arteries.

There was barely a sound, just the familiar faint gurgle as Faris lost consciousness, his hulking mass now resting sideways on the dirty concrete floor.

A few moments later, the Professor finished his coffee and calmly walked down the passageway on his left, apparently paying no mind as he passed a muscle-bound corpse in the corner of the alley.

Easy work indeed.

The man in the finely tailored dark suit stood at the agreed upon location in Place Jourdan and checked his Cartier watch.

17:31.

The Professor was late.

He turned to face the mirror in the corridor,

checking his hair, slicked-back with gel, then assumed his customary pose - hips jutted out over feet spread shoulder-width apart. He thrust his hands into his pockets, annoyed at the delay.

He was not accustomed to being made to wait.

Five minutes passed and the man in the dark suit had reached the limits of his patience.

But wait he would. He had questions that required answers from the Professor. Amsterdam had not gone exactly to plan, and now he would have to start over. But there were certain details that only the Professor could answer - - and then there was the question of the package...

When his call to Faris' mobile phone went unanswered, his irritation made the slightest shift toward preoccupation.

This was irregular. Most irregular.

Sensing the changing dynamics, the man in the suit made his way out to the street, heading towards his Mercedes and the driver waiting just around the corner.

And that's when it happened.

The dark van pulled up sharply with a screech in front of him. Two men jumped out the side door, and before the man in the suit could react, there was a hood over his head and he was pushed prone onto the van floor.

The sliding door slammed shut. And the van sped away into the evening Brussels traffic.

Mark Vashtan put down his phone, then leaned in close to Natalie, whispering the news.

It was done.

They'd have a meal in Brussels tonight, oysters and Champagne, then a main course of *sole meuniere*, paired with an exquisite bottle of *Chevalier-Montrachet Grand Cru*.

They celebrated late into the evening, but did not get drunk.

This time, they wanted to remember.

RIVIERA MAYA, MEXICO

P ete Strickland touched down in the quiet of early morning Cancun. The tourist swarms had yet to arrive, and the Yucatan air, already hot and humid, greeted him outside the arrivals gate with a welcoming embrace.

Bienvenidos.

Pete pushed past the few overzealous tour guides, and walked down to the curb, where he bought what was to be the first of many Caribbean beers, an ice-cold Sol from one of the little makeshift bars lining the outside of the terminal.

He was almost home.

Over the next few hours he'd make his way south, passing the resorts lining the coast and driving down past eco-chic Tulum and it's yoga retreats, then curling around the Sian Ka'an biosphere reserve, all the way to the little beach town of Xcalak on the Caribbean Sea.

From there he'd charter a private boat taking him the short distance along the coast and across the border into Belize's Ambergris Caye.

Finally, he was back.

He checked himself into the little crumbling cinderblock hotel near the water-taxi terminal and went up to his favourite private lounger on the roof, a dark bottle of Belikin beer in his hand.

He laid there for the better part of an hour, doing nothing, his mind completely blank. And then something, perhaps the arrival of that familiar far-off smell of rain in the air, turned his thoughts to the last time he was in Belize - and to his friend Angel Hernandez.

Goddamnitall, he thought to himself, *I sure hope it was worth it.*

That was the question he'd been asking himself as he'd made his way back down to Belize. Back to where it had all started.

Well, was it worth it?

He tried to keep score. The Catalan was dead, the Professor probably soon to follow - and a threat to the stability of Europe had been effectively neutralised.

Still, none of that would bring his friend back. Hernandez's death was on him. But then he remembered, he hadn't asked to be pulled back into the game. They'd forced his hand. It was never his choice.

It was never his choice.

And so Angel's death wouldn't be on his conscience. No, it certainly would not.

But he'd still miss him.

Fuck.

Trying to shake off the melancholy, Pete made his way down to Angelita's Hotel along the beach, wandering through the pastel-coloured bungalows and out to the hotel bar near the water's edge.

He took a seat at a bamboo stool, underneath the television tuned to the international news channel, and then motioned for the ponytailed bartender.

"Hey buddy, would you mind turning up the volume?"

It was a breaking news report from the continent:

...top European minister Jean Lemure, known among

his colleagues in Brussels for his expensively tailored dark suits, was arrested yesterday on wide-ranging corruption and conspiracy charges. Lemure, who had previously been in charge of various security and economic portfolios going back decades, was being held in an undisclosed location due to fears over his own safety...

Pete smiled just a little, "undisclosed location my ass..."

The ponytailed bartender, waiting for an order, didn't understand.

"Excuse me?"

"Ah, nothing..." Pete looked off into the sea, the slightest hint of contentment finally starting to push through to the surface.

"Can I get you something, sir?"

"You bet. How about a cold one in one of those frosty mugs you got there?"

"Right away, sir."

It was finally time to relax.

His beer arrived, in the opaque frozen mug that was the speciality of the house.

"Classy," he said to himself, "Well here's to you, Angel..."

He was just about to take a first sip when an old

man, face hidden under a Panama hat and behind vintage Persol sunglasses, sat down just to his left, where a lone palm tree bent crookedly out over the row of open stools.

That's when he heard it. Barely a muffled whisper floating on the ocean breeze.

"*It's all about human nature...*"

Pete turned, and felt his stomach clench slightly, his body's primal response to the latent sense of danger.

"What did you just say?"

The old man turned toward him, a gentle grin on his sunburned and scarless face.

"I said, it sure is a nice day"

Pete turned back out to face the blue waters of the Caribbean, and the waves breaking languidly on the reef just off the shore.

"Yeah, it sure is, isn't it..."

SYMI ISLAND, GREECE

One month later...

On the Dodecanese island of Symi, a short ferry ride from the port at Rhodes, two black-booted men with military style haircuts were making not-so-subtle inquiries about the older Italian gentleman who had recently taken up residence on the far side of the island.

It is true, the locals told them - they had heard of the man who walked with a cane. He usually kept to himself, wandering out occasionally for

an ouzo at the bar near the ancient Greek Ortho-
dox monastery of the Archangel Michael.

Yes, he would be there - they explained - where
else would he go? There is but one road leading
across the mountain and over to the harbour at
the monastery.

They would find him in one of the cluster of
fisherman's huts down a gravel path near the main
entrance to the church parking lot. There was a
small taverna down by the water there, and a peb-
ble beach popular with the local goats who wandered up to the seaside tables in search of the occasional morsel thrown their way.

Off to the left were the little cottages, spaced a
few metres apart just off the shoreline. There was
a small jetty there, and a handful of wooden fishing boats, painted blue and white, resting in the
shallow bend of the coast.

The taverna owner confirmed for them he was
there. In the 3rd hut down, with the turquoise
striped door.

The two men moved stealthily now down the narrow path to the Professor's hideaway. They had
him now. He was cornered, the cliff at the end of
the beach blocking any exit on foot.

Upon arriving at the turquoise-striped door, one
of the men rapped twice, before the second one
suddenly, and brutally, kicked open the wood-

framed portal.

They crept into the spartan interior, guns drawn, and found it empty except for the single bed in the corner and a small coffee table next to a tiny decrepit kitchen.

The dented and worn Italian-style Moka pot was still warm…

But the Professor was not there.

Instead they found only a golden ring, engraved with three tiny honeybees, lingering on the lone table.

A breeze blew in through the open shutters facing the jetty down on the beach, framing a perfect view of the dark blue sea…and the Turkish coast in the distance.

HELSINKI, FINLAND

3 years later...

Mark Vashtan had settled easily into his new life here in northern Europe.

Natalie had recently been promoted to station-chief in Tallinn, her career having truly taken off after the Catalan job. Finally, the powers that be were seeing her true talent.

And like he had always said, she was a natural.

The Helsinki post had been an easy job for him to accept, especially since Estonia was just a short two-hour ferry ride away. Close enough to stay in touch, but not too close to interfere with her professional ambitions.

It was a good compromise. She deserved to spread her wings. And anyway, they were both busy now focusing on a new threat. This time coming from an old enemy, as Russian sabre-rattling had finally started to make the policymakers in the West nervous.

It felt good to be here on the frontier of what seemed to be a new battle-line, and an emerging confrontation between East and West. And perhaps most importantly for Vashtan, it was this new challenge that had reinvigorated him, both personally and professionally.

Finally his head was clear, and he was back in the game.

It was a chilly late-afternoon in October and he was meeting his contact here in the city centre, in a very-crowded industrial-looking coffee shop (the Finns being prodigious consumers of caffeinated, roasted beverages).

Mark sat with a stylish pot of artisanal pour-over coffee as he waited for his contact to arrive, a surly Russian émigré named Boris.

Boris was the type of source who didn't say much,

Max Mitkevicius

but when he did it was usually something worth listening to.

When Boris arrived, punctual as always, he brusquely pushed his way through the crowd, immediately sat down with a thump and skipped the usual pleasantries. They weren't his style.

"Moscow is talking."

"Oh?"

"There's a name…"

Vashtan immediately felt an old but familiar twinge of uneasiness, his breathing now short and shallow.

Boris continued.

"Have you ever heard the name Leport?"

The colour suddenly drained from Vashtan's face, as the paralysing anxiety washed over him.

"Excuse me…"

"Leport. Arnau Leport."

He tried to wake from his private nightmare, but it was useless.

The Catalan was back.

Made in the USA
Columbia, SC
07 November 2019